The Amish Sermon

Vanessa Carlson

Published by Trellis Publishing, 2021.

This is a work of fiction. Similarities to real people, places, or events are entirely coincidental.

THE AMISH SERMON

First edition. July 8, 2021.

Copyright © 2021 Vanessa Carlson.

ISBN: 979-8224175390

Written by Vanessa Carlson.

THE AMISH SERMON

VANESSA CARLSON

Chapter 1

It was the end of the harvest season. The good Lord had blessed the community with a surplus of crops, ensuring that each and every family would make it through the winter, full and satisfied. Every member of the community had pulled their weight and it was this team effort that led to their success.

Now, it was time for some rest.

"I was thinking of making some chicken stew this evening. Would you like to join us for dinner?" Rebecca had her head resting on her fiancé's chest, listening to the soft whisper of his breath against her ear. Soon, they would be married, and she'd wake up every morning with his warmth beside her. Until then, all she could do was enjoy these fleeting moments.

"I can't," he said. "My father is returning tonight."

The air around the couple became thick enough to choke on. Matthew's father was a touchy subject. He had left the Amish community shortly after divorcing his wife. Divorce was almost unheard of within the faith. Those who instigated a divorce were often shunned from the community, becoming outcasts. Matthew's father was one of them.

"Returning?" questioned Rebecca. "Will your mother allow it?"

"He is staying with me."

"I see."

"Do you take issue with that?" Rebecca had been the one person to stay by his side during his parents' separation. She had offered him nothing but support and love, but Matthew could not help but notice a certain coldness to her voice. "I invited him to our wedding. I was hoping that he could give the sermon."

Rebecca bit her lower lip.

"What's wrong?"

"I do not think that my family will approve of him giving the sermon. He's been ousted from the community, Matthew..."

"But he remains my father," he countered. It was very rare that he lost his temper with his soon-to-be bride, but he could feel his blood boiling underneath the skin. "And I don't know why everyone treats him like such a bad guy. I mother had just as much to do with the divorce."

He released his hold on Rebecca and got to his feet, turning his back.

She frowned. It had not been her intention to upset him. "I'm sorry," she said as she attempted to turn him around. "I only know that my family will find fault with him giving the sermon and I thought I would save us both some grief by mentioning it beforehand."

Matthew sighed. "What about you? Do you want him to be there?"

"Of course," she answered. "You know how much I love your father. I always thought he was a charming and respectful individual."

"So then, what does it matter what anyone else thinks if we are both in agreement?"

Rebecca looked into Matthew's eyes and saw nothing but pure determination. He was going to get his father to say the sermon even if the whole world stood up against. "You're right," she said at last. "It shouldn't matter."

Matthew smiled. "I knew you would understand." He took her by the shoulders and drew her in, wrapping his arms around her. His embraced tightened as he caught her scent. It was as sweet as ever. His smile deepened. He still could not believe that this woman was to be his wife. Never in his wildest dreams did he think he would ever get this lucky. "Well, I should get going. I don't want to keep my father waiting."

Rebecca grabbed his hand before he could walk away. "Will I see you tomorrow?"

He leaned down and kissed the top of her head. "I will make sure of it," he promised. "It is becoming harder and harder to leave when you look at me like that." It was like Rebecca had tethered some sort of rope around his heart. She pulled on it and tugged him that much closer. Gently, he raised his hand to her cheek, brushing her skin with the tips of his fingers. "We only need to wait a little longer. Soon, we will be husband and wife."

"I cannot wait," whispered Rebecca, lost in the depths of his emerald eyes. "The days drag, and time passes by slower than molasses."

"Patience, my dear." He ran his fingers through her hair. "Our day will come."

With that, they both went their separate ways. Rebecca glanced over her shoulder, but Matthew was already gone. With a quick stride, he made it back to his home within a few minutes' time. His father was waiting by the door but before he could even raise his hand in greeting, he was intercepted by some of Rebecca's male relatives. Her father was the tallest of the ground. Next came Rebecca's brother, a young man with a permanent scowl etched onto his face. Off to the side stood his uncle, an old woodworker with weathered fingers. "What is the meaning of this?" hissed the brother. "You disgrace Rebecca by allowing this man into our community. He has no right to be here!"

"He is my father." It took a tremendous effort on Matthew's part to keep his voice under control. The last thing he wanted to do was sour the relationships he had formed with these men but, at the same time, he could not stand by and allow them to talk about his father as if he were some sort of monster. "And he'll be attending our wedding."

Rebecca's father stared at his future son-in-law with narrowed eyes. His lips were pressed together into a thin line.

"Does Lynita know about this?" asked the uncle. "She has a right to know."

"I intend to speak with her before the night is over." Matthew's father joined the conversation. Despite his reputation, he stood with an air of confidence. "You needn't worry about that."

"You've got a lot of nerve showing your face around here after what you did to Lynita." Rebecca's bother was seething. The anger had his face blotched with red.

"That is a matter between Lynita and me, son. Do not assume you know the whole story from the gossip you've heard."

Rebecca's bother looked like he was about to explode.

"Maybe we should head inside," said Matthew. He feared an altercation. Rebecca's bother was known for such outbursts. So, he navigated between them and took hold of his father, towing him toward the house while Rebecca's relative grumbled to themselves, eventually walking away.

Chapter 2

"Getting you to say that sermon at the wedding might prove harder than I thought..." Matthew whispered under his breath as he pulled at his hair, pacing the room.

"Perhaps coming back was a mistake," said Elmer, noting his son's agitation. "I am only causing trouble by being here."

"*I* want you to be here," Matthew responded. "Despite everything that has happened, you remain my father. That will never change. And for that reason, I want you to be there when I marry the love of my life."

Elmer smiled. He could remember the days when Matthew was only a boy. Oh, how he had pinned over sweet little Rebecca. He had made up every sort of excuse just to see her. Even then, it was clear to see that one day they would end up together, living out their happily ever after.

"But there are some things that I want answered." Matthew had stopped his pacing and now stood in the middle of the room, unmoving. "Why did you divorce mother?"

He had been waiting for this question. It was painful to put his reasoning into words, but he understood that his son had a right to know the truth. There was no telling what kind of rumors had circulated through the community, muddling what had really happened. "It came to a point where we were both happier when we were away from one another. Together, we'd do nothing but fight. I could see the misery weighing down on your mother. She was no longer the woman I had married, and I was to blame for that." He moved toward the window and cracked it open, needing the fresh air to continue. "So, I did what was best for her and left. I am sure she's much happier now that I'm out of her hair."

Matthew shook his head. "I don't think so. She's alone now. And when I talk to her, it's like she's not even there. Her mind seems to be elsewhere. I think that maybe she's thinking of you."

"That can't be," said Elmer. "She was glad to see me go."

"Things change as time passes."

Elmer wanted to believe that his son was right but at the same time, he did not want to get his hopes up. He still loved Lynita with all his heart and wanted nothing more than to go back to the way things were when they were first husband and wife.

"All I ask is that you talk to her. Make amends for the two of you will need to get along during the wedding."

"And if she doesn't want to talk?"

"Keep on trying until she stops to listen." Matthew placed a hand on his father's shoulder, squeezing it in an act of encouragement. "I know it won't be easy."

Elmer nodded. "But it must be done."

"She expects me for dinner tonight. Come alone."

"Uninvited?" Elmer was struck by the image of his late-wife hitting him with a frying pan the second he showed up at her door.

"Yes." Matthew left no room for argument in his voice. Without looking back, he left his house and started down the path toward his family home. It wasn't very far but even so, the whispers followed them. Women who were out gathering laundry from clotheslines brought their heads together and pointed in Elmer's direction. He quickened his pace but that did not stop the stares.

They couldn't have reached Lynita's house soon enough. As they waited for her to answer the door, Elmer looked around. He hadn't been gone very long and already the paint was starting to chip. The window boxes were full of weeds. Of course, he couldn't blame his ex-wife. No doubt, it was difficult for her to maintain an entire household on her own. Back when they had been married, they had divided all the chores evenly down the middle. That was no longer the case. Guilt thickened at his throat until it became impossible for him to breathe.

It was then that Lynita showed up at the door, wearing an apron and a bit of flour on her cheek. Elmer felt his chest seize up at the sight of her. He hadn't realized how much he had truly missed her until that very moment. "Lynita…" he spoke her name like it was a prayer. He dared to take a step in her direction.

She crossed her arms and tapped her foot. "What is *he* doing here?" she asked of her son. "If I recall correctly, you were the only one that I invited to dinner."

"I thought that he could join us. You always make more than enough food."

"I do not want him inside my home."

"Mother…"

"You don't understand," she snapped. "You don't understand the pain – the humiliation – that this man caused me."

"Mother, please. I need you to breathe. All I want is for us to discuss the wedding. It needn't be anything more than that."

"Don't tell me that you've invited him to the wedding?"

"I have." Matthew was trying to make his way into the house, but his mother was shielding the entrance with her body. "And I intend to have him say the sermon."

"The sermon?" she recoiled like someone who had just suffered a tremendous blow. "You've lost your mind!" And with that, she slammed the door.

Matthew called after his mother, but she refused to answer.

"I think she has made her opinion quite clear. We do nothing but waste our time by being here," said Elmer. He did not wait for his son but walked away for he could not bear to look at his old home for another moment. It was too painful to stare at everything he had lost.

Chapter 3

"How did it go last night?" Rebecca was busy making some flower arrangements for the wedding when Matthew arrived at her home.

"Terribly," he answered.

She handed him some flowers to keep him busy. "That bad, huh?"

"I didn't expect to have him welcomed back with open arms, but I didn't expect total hostility either."

"What happened?" Rebecca flinched when she saw her fiancé crushing the petals of a white rose. Those were extremely difficult to come across, but she didn't think it appropriate to point out his blunder when he was so upset. There were plenty of other flowers.

"Well, first off, I was confronted by your brother, father, and uncle."

"So, I heard." She had gotten an earful from all of them the second they saw her that night. They had tried to convince her that marrying Matthew was a mistake – that he was bound to follow in his father's footsteps – but she loved Matthew, and nothing would ever change that. "They were telling me all sorts of awful things."

Matthew stopped what he was doing and looked across the table at his betrothed. "What sort of things?"

She shook her head. "I rather not repeat them."

He sunk into his chair. "Everyone seems to think that my father is some sort of criminal but he's truly a good man. He never meant to hurt my mother. They simply drifted apart. Why should he be so deeply hated for something out of his control? Clearly, the good Lord played a part in this divorce as he plays a part in everything."

Rebecca reached across the table and squeezed his hand. "I know. Trust me, your father practically raised me as his own daughter. I have seen nothing but his kindness shine through. His divorce won't have changed his character."

Matthew felt like her words had lifted a weight from his soul. Rebecca always knew how to make him feel better. "So, you won't mind if he gives the sermon at the wedding?"

"Of course not," she answered. "I'd be honored to have him there. His sermons are always so beautiful."

"That's why I want him there. My father always speaks from the heart whereas the prophet—"

"The prophet is a well-bred man brought up in the faith." It was Rebecca's mother who had interrupted Matthew from finishing. She was holding a rather large bowl against her hip and stirring it to an almost violent degree. "And I will not tolerate any insults—"

"I was not insulting the man," countered Matthew. Getting nowhere with the flower arrangement, he abandoned the project and got to his feet. "I was only saying that his sermons—"

"Are excellent," she interrupted a second time. "He always has me hanging on every single word." She punctuated every syllable and Matthew felt them like a blow to the gut. There was no way that he would ever change this woman's mind.

"Unfortunately, you won't be listening to the prophet's *excellent* sermon during *our* wedding." There was a pause as Matthew waited for his wife-to-be to join him underneath his outstretched arm. Rebecca eyed her mother who was growing redder and redder by the second. She was just about the color of a ripened tomato when Rebecca got up and shuffled towards her future groom. Rebecca loved her mother, yes, but Matthew was right. The prophet was always dull with his sermons while Elmer brought life to every single sentence. Bias was getting in the way of proper judgment,

"He's right, mother."

She stared at her daughter, mouth slightly ajar like she was a fish out of water, gasping for breath. She blinked a few times like doing so might change the scene before her. "I cannot believe this..." she murmured with her hand clasped over her heart. "My very own daughter defending a divorced man!"

"Mother—" started Rebecca, wanting to defend her position but her mother would hear none of it. She had already turned on her heels and disappeared into the kitchen.

Matthew frowned. "I do not want to come between you two."

"No," said Rebecca. "I want your father to say the sermon so that everyone can understand that he's still the same man that we all knew and loved."

***

Despite every bit of resistance, the couple stuck to their resolution. Elmer stood behind a wooden podium with a few sheets of paper in his hand. They trembled slightly but when he spoke, his voice was strong and full of confidence.

"We are brought here today to celebrate the love shared between my son, Matthew, and his lovely bride, Rebecca. As you can all imagine, I've known Matthew all his life." A few people in the crowd chuckled at his joke only to be stared down by the glares of others. "I was there with Lynita when Matthew was born and I can say without a doubt, that it was the happiest day of my life."

The glares intensified.

Sitting in the front row, Lynita scowled. The lines on her face were etched so deep that they threatened to become permanent.

"But I think Matthew's happiest day was when he noticed Rebecca for the very first time. If I remember correctly, Rebecca was helping her mother with a bit of laundry. They were by the river. Matthew was so transfixed by Rebecca that he stumbled straight into the water. When I pulled him out, he looked like a drowned cat."

Again, a few people dared to chuckle. There seemed to be more of them.

"So, I want us to celebrate their innocence and the love that they share because it is through this love that they'll find salvation." He held out his arms, motioning toward the congregated community. "Scripture tells us to live in harmony – to treat those within the community as brother and sister – to do no harm to those created by the hand of God..." As he continued, his voice seemed to take on a life of its own. It reverberated through the chapel and penetrated into the heads of all those that listened.

Suddenly, they felt the burning of shame. The flames licked at their seats until they could barely keep still. Many of the members fidgeted, looking at the neighbors, hoping that they were not alone in the way they felt.

"Now, I cannot speak on the Lord's behalf, but I think we can all agree that we were brought here today for a very special reason."

Chapter 4

Rebecca wiped the tear from her eye. Never before had words touched her so deeply. It was like they had been written upon her heart, becoming more deeply embedded with every beat.

Matthew beamed at his father. He had proven himself in front of the entire congregation. There wasn't a single person who could argue against the raw emotion he had put into his speech or the truth of what he said.

Knowing this, Lynita sought him out during the reception. "Elmer?" The first time she called his name, it became lost in the din of the crowd. Her cheeks reddened when she saw people looking her way. For a moment, she reconsidered the conversation. Perhaps the sermon had been nothing but an act.

But the words came echoing into her mind once more. Elmer was not the vile man she had made him out to be in the heartbreak of their separation. He was the same old Elmer she had always known – the father of her child – the first and only man she had ever loved. If she allowed him to leave, would she ever get another chance to apologize?

"No," she thought. *"I have got to make things right. I cannot let things remain the way they are now."* Lynita held onto that resolve as she stepped forward. The field was full of jovial dancers. She shuffled her way through them, losing sight of her ex-husband along the way. Once on the other side, she scanned the tables, but he was nowhere to be found. It was like he had disappeared.

"Looking for me?" came a familiar whisper.

Lynita jumped right out of her skin. She hadn't expected him to sneak up on her like that. Yet, it was something he was known to do. He had done it about a million times during their marriage. In those days, he'd wrap his arms around her waist and bury his face against her neck. Just the thought was enough to bring back the honeycomb scent of her hair. He breathed it in as he caught her, preventing her from falling.

"Easy now," he warned. "Wouldn't want you getting hurt on our son's wedding night." He held her a little tighter than he had intended to. Without thinking, he pulled her close so that their faces were mere inches apart. "Was there something that you wanted to say?" he asked, his voice sounding distant and strange.

She nodded but her mouth was too dry to respond.

The song ended.

Elmer stepped even closer, now holding out his hand in invitation. "Would you like to dance?" He did not let himself believe that she would ever say 'yes.' Instead, he steeled himself against the rejection that was sure to come.

"I would," she said.

Now it was Elmer that looked like a fish out of water. "I..." he stammered, unable to string together the words needed for a coherent sentence.

Lynita smiled knowingly. The band started up again and old habits fell into place. Their feet moved with the rhythm, propelling their bodies along the field. Soon, they were lost in the crowd – just another happy couple underneath the stars.

It felt like time had come to a standstill. The world around them had ceased to exist as they stood there, forehead to forehead. "Whatever happened to us?" asked Lynita. "We used to have it all and then one day, things just weren't the same. It was like we had become strangers inside our own home."

"I can't tell you when it happened," answered Elmer. "I only know that it did and that I could not stand it."

"Is that why you chose to leave?"

"I chose to leave because I could see that I was causing you pain. It was written in your eyes. Every time that you looked at me, it felt like something was stabbing into my heart. I thought that walking away would save you from that pain."

Lynita rested her head on his chest. His heartbeat was just as she remembered it. "You're a fool."

"Excuse me?"

"You heard what I said."

"And why am I a fool?"

"Because you convinced yourself that I no longer loved you when that's the furthest thing from the truth. I don't think that I will ever stop loving you for as long as I live."

Elmer stopped dancing. "Do you mean that?"

"I do. And I would very much like for us to start again. We'll clean off the slate and –" Lynita could not finish what she was saying for Elmer had suddenly cupped both cheeks in his hands and kissed her.

Feeling her lips against his own was like coming home. As the kiss continued, he felt a warmth spreading throughout his insides. The loneliness that had once gripped him like a vice was gone. He could smile once again.

And that's exactly what he did. It was a wheelbarrow smile that stretched from ear to ear. "I love you, Lynita," he whispered, still unbelieving of the fact that his ex-wife had come to forgive him.

"I love you too, Elmer."

Chapter 5

"Do you see what I see?" Matthew was sitting on a tree trunk, his new wife on his lap.

"Hmm?" Rebecca, ever the fiend for sweets, was busy biting into a shortbread cookie made by one of her neighbors. A few crumbs lingered on her lips. Unable to resist, Matthew leaned forward and claimed them for himself.

The quick peck on the lips became much more than that as soon as his love for Rebecca swept through his veins, pumping straight into his heart and making it work ten times as fast. He kissed her a little harder as if his life depended on keeping his lips firmly planted against hers.

By the time Matthew released his hold, Rebecca was a bright shade of pink. She was breathing hard, trying to stop herself from floating away. "What were you saying...?" The kiss had left her in a sort of daze.

Matthew chuckled. "Look," he pointed at the dancing couples. "If I am not mistaken, that would be my father leading my mother in dance."

Rebecca had to shift her position to see exactly what Matthew was talking about but sure enough, there they were. "Do you think this means that they have gotten past their divorce?"

"I certainly hope so," said Matthew. "For I want nothing more than to have my children spoiled by both sets of grandparents."

"Thinking about children already?" she asked. "Isn't it a bit too early for such things?"

"I don't think so." Matthew took her by the hips and stood up. It seemed like he would bring her over to the crowd to continue their dancing but instead, he laced their fingers together and pulled her toward the river.

The flow of it was calm that night. It lapped gently at the rocks.

"Do you remember when we were young?" Matthew stopped at the riverbank and wrapped his arms around her waist from behind. "Back then, I used to think that you were the prettiest girl in the world?"

"And now?" Rebecca turned her head to look at him.

"And now I think you are the most beautiful girl in the world."

The blush that still lingered upon her cheeks brightened in color.

Smiling, Matthew leaned in for another kiss only to lose his balance. He tried to steady himself by grabbing hold of Rebecca, but it did not help. Instead, they both went tumbling towards the water, landing with a loud *splash!*

Rebecca flailed her arms about. The fabric of her dress was weighing her down and pulling her towards the bottom of the river.

Before the water could close in over the top of her head, Matthew grabbed her by the arms and hoisted her out. "Are you alright?" he asked as soon as he laid her down on a nearby patch of grass.

She started laughing but Matthew did not understand why. Had the coldness of the water caused her to lose her mind.

"Rebecca?"

"It's just funny," she said.

"What is?"

"The way you're looking at me. You wore the same look when you saved me the first time. I can't quite explain it but it's as if you would keel over if something were to happen to me."

"That's because I would," he answered with all seriousness. "I don't think you understand how much you truly mean to me." He brushed a wet strand of hair from her face and tucked it behind her ear. "You're the reason why my heart keeps beating. You're the first person that I think about when I wake up in the morning and when I fall asleep, it is you that I dream about."

Rebecca was no longer laughing. She was caught in the intensity of his gaze. "Matthew..."

"And I want you to know that I cannot control the future. I cannot promise you that I won't follow in my father's footsteps. There are sure to be fights. And there will certainly be times where our relationship becomes difficult. I do not doubt that things will happen, but I can tell you this: whatever happens, I will always be there. I will be there to hold your hand when you give birth to our first child and I will be there when we are both old and grey."

Rebecca placed her finger against his lips to stop him from talking. "You needn't prove yourself to me. I wouldn't have married you if I thought you were an unfaithful man who would leave me at the drop of a hat. Today has been the best day of my life. Your father delivered a wonderful sermon. I was able to marry the love of my life. And at the end of the day, the community was able to come together and enjoy God's blessing. What more could I ever ask for?" She settled into the grass and motioned for Matthew to join her.

He did, placing one arm around her as they looked up at the twinkling stars. They seemed brighter than ever before. Matthew smiled to himself because despite all the worries he had carried, everything had worked out in the end. He was laying beside the woman of his life and somewhere, his father was making amends with his mother. "Cheers to a bright and happy future," he said, lifting his arm in an imaginary toast.

"Cheers, indeed," agreed Rebecca with a giggle.

Epilogue

Two years later.

Rebecca was in the backyard, hanging some clothes to dry. Her feet were swollen, and her body was reaching its breaking point but even so, her unborn child seemed content with staying inside the safety of her stomach.

"What do you think you're doing?" Lynita came rushing towards the pregnant woman with a shake of her head. "You shouldn't be straining yourself like this. The doctor has recommended that you stay inside and rest."

"If I remain inside that house any longer, I am sure to lose my mind. Being idle and staring at walls –"

Lynita could sympathize with her daughter-in-law. Her own pregnancy had been a long one and towards the end of it, she wanted nothing more than for it to end. "I know, dear, but it cannot be helped."

Just then, Matthew and his father emerged from the barn with a slaughtered goat. The animal had been skinned and hung by its feet on a long pole, carried on either side by the two men. "Where shall we put this?" called Elmer. "Have you got the fire started yet?"

"Not quite. There's only so much that I can do at one time!"

Rebecca and her husband exchanged looks. They were sure the older couple was about to go at it but to their surprise, they managed to hold their tongues. Their relationship was far from perfect, but they were working hard to improve it.

"Alright then, let me help you with that," offered Elmer.

"That would be nice." Lynita smiled in response. She joined her husband and together they went off and gathered some firewood. The divorce had long been forgiven by the faith and they were once again living underneath the same roof. Doing so caused a bit of friction but they were learning to respect and love each other in a whole new way.

"Do you think today will be the day?" asked Lynita. "I am starting to worry. The full moon has come and gone. The baby should have been here by now."

"He will arrive when he is ready to arrive," said Elmer. "There is no need to rush the poor tyke."

"Think of his mother!"

"Rebecca is a strong young woman. I am not worried about her."

Lynita clicked her tongue against the roof of her mouth. "I don't think you realize what it takes to bring a child into this world. Contrary to what men might think –"

"Dear," he interrupted. "I did not mean anything of the sort. There is no need for you to get all riled up. I just think that Rebecca is capable of handling the situation."

Lynita reminded herself to breathe. With her head a little clearer, she nodded. "You're right. I am sorry that I misunderstood you." And just like that, a fight had been avoided. Had it been a few years earlier, they would have been screaming at each other. Now, no more. Those days were over and Lynita had no intention of going back to those times of anger and frustration.

"I think that's more than enough firewood, don't you think?" Elmer cradled an armful of logs.

"More than enough, I think," she answered.

When they returned to the yard, Rebecca had taken a seat underneath the shade of a nearby tree. She smiled and waved.

"Ah, there you two are," greeted Matthew. "I was wondering whether you had gotten lost."

"Lost?" quipped Elmer. "I know these woods better than the back of my hand."

Lynita waved off his boasting but there was a slight smile playing on her lips.

Soon, there was a bonfire in place. It burned with a welcoming heat. The smell of burning wood filled the air. Rebecca's smile deepened for she had always found the smell of firewood a comforting one.

Together, the men worked on hoisting the goat above the fire. The fat sizzled against the flames. "Looks like we'll be eating well tonight." It was Rebecca's father. Her side of the family walked onto the property carrying bowls filled with side dishes.

Rebecca felt her stomach rumble. Suddenly, she came to realize that she was starving. Her child gave a kick of excitement. A gasp escaped her lips. A second later, Matthew was there by her side for she had doubled over, clutching her midsection. "What is the matter?" he asked. "Is it the baby?"

"Yes..." she breathed. "I..." She could barely keep herself standing. Her knees knocked together as her legs became like jelly.

Matthew did not wait another moment. He took her in his arms and brought her inside. The rest of the family followed save for Rebecca's brother who had dashed off to fetch the community doctor.

"You're doing great," Matthew whispered as he eased her onto the bed. "I just need you to keep breathing for me, okay? Just keep breathing. In and out." The advice was as much for her as it was for himself. Never before had he felt so nervous. For months, he knew that this day would come but now that it had arrived, it was like he was caught in some sort of dream.

"Don't leave."

"I won't," promised Matthew as he took hold of her hand. She held it with such a tightness that Matthew feared it would snap right in two. Although that would certainly be a small price to pay if it meant the safe birth of his first child. "Do you think it will be a boy or a girl?" he asked her in hopes that it would distract her from the pain she felt.

"It does not matter," she answered through gritted teeth. "So long as it's healthy."

Matthew leaned down and kissed the top of her head. "I have faith that it will be."

***

After what felt like an eternity, a tiny baby boy was finally heard. His cry echoed through the entire room. "Isn't he precious..." whispered Lynita. "I cannot believe that we are standing here as grandparents when Matthew's birth feels like it happened just yesterday."

"I know what you mean," agreed Elmer as he kept his eyes fixed on the bundle of blankets being passed around the room. Soon, his grandson was nestled against the crook of his arm. Lynita fawned over him, cooing the entire time. The infant grabbed hold of her finger.

Elmer felt his heart melt into a puddle. He had once thought that Matthew's birth would forever be the happiest day of his life, but he had been proven wrong. Being here with his wife, there really wasn't anything better. "Welcome to the family," he whispered. "And God bless you for all your days as he has blessed mine."

AMISH SUNSET

NANCY MANN

Chapter I

Rain decorated the grassy fields of Lancaster County. The sky was a cloud grey, the sun remaining absent as the county mourned for the loss of William Bradshire, a carpenter that had been known throughout the county for his kindness and love towards the people around him.

Friends and family had gathered in the county's cemetery for William's funeral, one of the mourners being William's love, Mary Lee Warner. Out of everyone there, Mary was the most damaged from it. William's parents had passed on early in his life due to illnesses and the remaining family he had weren't as close. If anything, Mary was the only one there who truly was family to him.

As Bishop David spoke about his memories with William, Mary thought to herself how God could do such a thing, to take away an innocent being this early in his life. William was only in his mid-twenties, like Mary. He had so much to experience in his life, but it was stripped away from him so early due to the accident.

"If anyone has anything to say, speak now." Bishop David said, stepping back and letting anyone step forward to speak.

There was a long pause, silence being present as Mary thought to herself. Eventually, she took a step forward, standing in front of the casket as she let out a depressed sigh.

"William...had a beautiful soul," Mary said quietly, holding onto a wildflower, "a soul that I have yet to find in any other human being."

Everyone was watching her speak, seeing what Mary had in her hand and what she had to say about William being gone.

"I can't imagine not meeting him in my life...all the memories we've made together...all the laughter, the love...I'm going to miss it." Mary spoke as tears ran down her cheeks. "I don't know if I will find another William in my life."

Some of William's family members began to have tears fall too as they listened to Mary's words about their lost kin. Mary soon stepped back from the casket, having finished speaking on the behalf of William's death. Bishop David soon stepped forward again, wiping some tears from his own eyes.

"Thank you Mary...I will say, before I close in prayer, that it will be difficult to find another William in our lives." Bishop David said to Mary before opening his Bible.

Verses from the Bible were soon spoken out loud, everybody bowing their heads in prayer as Bishop David spoke. While everyone listened, Mary wasn't listening to the verses, in fact, she was in her own mind at this point.

"Why God...why would you take William away from me?" Mary thought to herself. "William didn't even get half way into his life...why would you take him now?"

As she struggled with the idea of William passing on, Bishop David finished reading the verses, quietly speaking the word amen as he closed his Bible, everybody soon leaving the scene of the funeral, letting the casket to be lowered into the grave. While the casket lowered, Mary was the only one present, witnessing her love's final presence on the surface of Earth.

In regards to funeral traditions of the Amish, flowers were not placed on the casket. For Mary though, traditions meant nothing to her in this occasion. She took the wildflower that she was holding in her hand and tossed it down into the undug grave, letting it land on the coffin before the gravediggers began to bury the coffin.

"I love you so much William." Mary said as the coffin soon disappeared from the soil piling on top. Tears continued to fall onto the soil as she left the site of the funeral.

Chapter II

Several years later...the county had returned back to its normal ways, except for Mary. Ever since William passed away, Mary wasn't her old self. Her old cheerful personality had passed on as well, leaving her a closed up, emotionless woman in her mid-twenties.

She tried to return back to a normal life by going to church, seeing if God might be able to help her find peace, but the more she went the church, the more she began to question God. At times, she would find herself being angry at God for taking William away this early in his life. Eventually, Mary stopped going to church, which brought the concern of Bishop David, leading him to go to Mary's home.

Her house was a little way from town, being near one of the farms. She lived in a large house that belonged to William and his parents. Now that William passed on, Mary now owned the house and lived in it by herself.

Bishop David knocked on the front door, waiting for it to be opened. It took a few knocks before the door finally opened, Mary standing there in a stone grey dress.

"Yes?" Mary quietly said, looking at him with her expressionless face.

"May I come in?" Bishop David asked softly, his expression being hopeful that she would accept his request.

Mary let out a quiet sigh before she nodded, stepping out of the way for Bishop David to come in.

"Thank you...Mary." He said, soon walking into her home, looking around.

Mary shut the door behind Bishop David, walking past him and sitting down on a chair in the living room, continuing what she was doing before he knocked. When Bishop David sat down across from her, he noticed that she was knitting a quilt.

"Oh...I see that you've been busy with making a quilt." Bishop David said, giving Mary a gentle smile.

"Quilts. I've been busy making quilts." She said quickly, pointing in the corner to a basket of several quilts.

Bishop David was surprised by the amount of quilts she had made. "That's quite the number of quilts Mary." He said with a small laugh after.

Mary raised her eyebrows as she continued to knit the quilt. "I've found that work is one of the few things that keeps me from thinking about the past." She said softly, not making eye contact with Bishop David.

"Oh...well...if that's what helps you find peace." He said quietly, rubbing the back of his neck before he finally decided to talk about why he wanted to talk to her. "Mary...I'm worried about you."

She heard Bishop David, stopping for a second before she continued knitting the quilt. "Why?" Mary questioned him.

"I'm concerned for you because you haven't been going to church for months." Bishop David finally said, looking at her with a worried expression. "You were always an avid church-goer when William..." He said before realizing what he said, stopping in mid-sentence.

Mary immediately looked up when Bishop David brought up William, her knitting ceasing before she let out a sigh of disbelief escape her lips. She set the quilt and knitting needle down. "Please, do not ever bring up William to me again when comparing me to then and now." Mary said, her voice trembling as she had grown an upset expression.

Bishop David had become silent as he listened to Mary finally speak to him.

"I'm no longer the Mary from then because of the events that happened, and if you want to visit me and tell me how I use to love church and that you're concerned with me not being there on Sundays, then don't even speak, you're wasting your breath." Mary said to him, her eyes staring into his intensely.

Bishop David heard everything she was saying before he let out a sigh of sympathy. "I'm sorry Mary that you're like this...I didn't come here today to chastise you about not attending church. I came here because I'm really concerned for what you've become. I want happiness for you, I want you to have that cheerful personality that everybody knew you for." He said softly, standing up from sitting, looking down at her. "Always remember Mary, we all face events in life that we don't want, but it's all a part of God's plan for something greater."

Mary just glared at him the whole time he spoke, not even acknowledging the things he said. "I would like you to leave."

Bishop David heard her request and nodded softly, walking away from where they were at and leaving the house.

She had watched him leave through the windows before she finally reached for her knitting needles and quilt, continuing to knit as she thought about what he said about God having a plan for everyone. To her, God's plan was killing William and taking away something that she loved most in the world, when she didn't have anyone else.

"Forget God." Mary said to herself quietly, having completely lost faith and love in God.

Chapter III

One stormy night soon had arrived in Lancaster County. Rain had arrived over the town and fields, the sound of sharp pellets hitting the roofs and windows of each building. The window whirled between each building, the sounds of wind wailing could be heard by anyone who was awake.

While the storm stayed present in the county, Mary was asleep in her bed, although she wasn't sleeping soundly. The red-headed woman was having a nightmare, causing her to toss back and forth in her sleep before some sort of sound interrupted her slumber.

KNOCK KNOCK KNOCK

Mary sat right up from her bed like a vampire in a coffin, rubbing her eyes. "What on Earth?" She said to herself, looking around the room as she wondered what caused her to wake up.

KNOCK KNOCK KNOCK

This time, the red-head heard the solution to the noise. "Who could be at my door in the middle of the night?" Mary got out of her bed, wrapping her blanket around herself to cover her nightgown. She made her way down the stairs of her home before seeing the front door. Once she got to the door, she slowly opened it, seeing who it was.

There was a man, about her age, with a young daughter about six-years-old. They were wet from head to toe, shivering as they looked at Mary.

"Please...do you have room in your home for my child and I? We come from far away to Lancaster County...we have no home, no food." The man said, his tone being a desperate one.

Mary had no idea that this was what waited for her on the other side of the door. "I...Well..." She looked at the two before she finally nodded quickly, stepping out of the way.

"Oh thank you...thank you!" The man said happily and emotionally. He quickly moved inside, Mary shutting the door behind the two. Even though they were inside, away from the rain, they still were shivering in the dark home. Mary saw how cold they were and immediately knew what they needed.

She quickly went over to the fireplace in the living room, taking two logs that were on the side of the hearth in a pile and putting them inside the fireplace. After a few attempts of trying to get a fire started, she eventually managed to do so, an orange glow illuminating the living room.

Once the man saw the fire, he moved his daughter close to the fireplace, trying to get her as warm as possible. Mary saw what he was trying to do and quickly went over to the eight-year-old, wrapping her blanket around the child. The man soon began to dry off her daughter while at the same time trying to get her warm.

"There you go...nice and warm now. Away from the cold rain." He said quietly to his daughter, holding her close as he sat in front of the fireplace with her.

The daughter shivered still, but the warmth from the fire and the blanket caused the shivering to decrease as the time went by.

Mary stood behind the two, watching them and making sure that they were okay. "Are you warm enough?" She asked them, having held one of the quilts she had made in her hands to give to the man.

"Yes...thank you kind miss." He said quietly, holding his daughter close before taking the quilt from Mary, wrapping it around himself.

With the two warming themselves up from the fire, Mary decided to grab another quilt for herself before sitting down on her couch. She wrapped the quilt around her body so she could be warm too. Since she now had two "guests" in her home, she didn't want to go upstairs, back to bed, with the knowledge that two strangers were downstairs in her home, two people who she had no idea who they were.

"Maybe they're thieves," Mary thought to herself, studying the two strangers. "Although...she looks pretty young to be a thief." She finally decided to speak up, wanting to figure out who they were. "Where did you two come from?"

The man looked back at her, hearing her question before he began to reply to her. "We came from Somerset County." The man answered, still trying to warm up his daughter.

"Oh...that's far from here." Mary replied, sitting down on her couch, looking at the man.

"It very much is..." The man nodded, looking at her. "Do you know if there's any housing here in Lancaster County?"

Mary heard her question before she shrugged. "I'm not too sure. Are you looking for a place to stay?"

The man nodded, looking down at his daughter. She had fallen into slumber and had a warm expression on her face and had stopped shivering, indicating she was no longer freezing. "Yes."

She heard him and asked some more questions in order to get to know him. "Why Lancaster County? I'm sure there's plenty of other settlements along the way."

"I just," The man began to say, rubbing the back of his neck nervously, "I don't know...I guess I've heard a lot of great things about Lancaster. Figured that it would be a great place for my daughter to grow up in."

Mary nodded when he stated that it'd be a good place for his daughter to grow up in. "Lancaster really is a nice place to grow up in...a good place to start a fam-" she began to say before stopping when she was about to say "family." It reminded her of what she has always wanted to have and that made her think of William and her. "Well, it's a good place to meet nice and caring people."

The man saw her reaction when she was talking about family, but decided not to question it in order to remain polite. "That's good to hear...by the way," the man began to say, looking at her once again, "what is your name?"

She heard him and replied softly. "Mary...my name is Mary Lee Warner."

When the man heard her, he smiled softly. "That's a beautiful name."

Mary smiled softly when he complimented her name. "What about you? What's your name?"

"Robert." He said quietly, before looking down at his daughter, gently stroking her hair. "The little one is Miriam."

Chapter IV

The next morning had arrived, the rain was now gone, the only trace of rain being the puddles in the dirt.

Mary decided to help Robert and Miriam out by going down to the church to see Bishop David could help them out.

Entering the church, there were only a few people present in the pews, praying to the Lord about whatever comes to their attention. Bishop David was not preaching, considering it was a Tuesday, so chances were he was at his home.

"Doesn't look like he's here." Mary said, turning around and leading Robert and Miriam out.

"Who are we looking for exactly?" Robert said, holding his daughter's hand as they walked towards Bishop David's house.

"We're looking for David, Lancaster County's bishop. He might be able to help you out with moving here." Mary replied, reaching the bishop's house before knocking on the door. Not too long after the knock, the door opened, Bishop David standing there.

"Mary?" He said, a little surprised. "What brings you here today?"

Mary explained the whole story to him, telling the bishop that Robert and Miriam showed up in the middle of the night, needing a place to stay and that they wanted to move to Lancaster.

"I see..." Bishop David said quietly, scratching his beard as he thought about it. "Unfortunately, there isn't any houses available right now."

Mary heard the news and let out a quiet groan. "So where will they stay if they don't have a home?"

Bishop David heard her before looking at the two, looking at Mary again. "Can I talk to you privately Mary?"

Mary was confused as to why, but nodded as she stepped inside the bishop's house. "What did you want to talk to me about?"

Bishop David looked at her before he let out a quiet sigh. "I wanted to talk to you privately about where they're going to stay. I believe they should continue living at your house until a new house can be built here in the county."

She listened to what he said before hearing his statement about the two staying at her home. "What? No. I can't have people living at my house."

Bishop David gave her a confused look. "Why not? You have one of the biggest houses here in Lancaster County. You're not living with anyone. There's plenty of room in the house for someone."

"Because, I don't have enough food to feed two more people. I don't want to start housing people." Mary was quick to say, folding her arms. "I can't let strangers come into my home and make themselves acquainted to the hou-"

"Mary." Bishop David interrupted, clearly showing he was getting irritated with her. "Enough with the excuses. I'm not going to force you to let them in. I'm only suggesting you give the two of them a home. It's not permanent, but where else are they going to go?" He asked Mary, looking at her with a serious expression. "They can't move into anyone else's home. They all have families, rather large ones too."

She listened to him, looking into his eyes as she thought about everything he was saying. Bishop David was right in many ways. Most families in the county had large families, homes that were already crowded. With Mary's house, it was just her. He even said that it wasn't permanent, so it'd be something that Mary didn't have to deal with for too long.

"I guess...I could have them stay for a little while." Mary finally admitted, realizing that she could be a little generous.

"Thank you Mary." Bishop David said before leading her back outside, now facing Robert. "We will discuss adding a house whenever I meet my colleagues. Until we can get a house added to the county, you'll have to stay with Mary for the time being."

Robert listened to what Bishop David said, nodding softly. "Okay, thank you."

Bishop David smiled softly, heading back into the house before closing the door.

Robert and Miriam turned toward Mary, looking at her. "So...are we going to back to the nice lady's house?" Miriam asked her father.

Mary heard her and couldn't help but smile. "Yes...yes you are."

Robert watched the two interact before he couldn't help but smile, seeing this stranger being so nice to his daughter.

"Alright. Let's head back to the house so I can get a room prepped up for you two." Mary said, clapping her hands together when she knew what she needed to do.

Chapter V

A couple of months passed by in Mary's household. The two strangers that had showed up on her doorstep were now friends of hers, having brightened up the household little by little. As Mary got to know Robert, he started feeling more and more comfortable around him, the two even joking around with each other.

With Miriam, she started to look up towards Mary as a mother figure, every now and then the little girl called Mary mom. Mary would hear this and laugh, finding it humorous that Robert's daughter called her mom.

While everyone was getting along just fine, Mary started to remember William again, every time she looked at Robert. There was something about Robert that reminded her of William. It might've been the way he made her laugh or the way he showed kindness to people. Whatever it was, Mary could see William through Robert, which made her think about if she found another William in her life.

It was now 6 PM and Robert and Miriam had finished eating dinner with Mary. When they finished, Robert decided to take Miriam to bed, since she started dozing off during dinner. Once she was in bed, she was out cold.

"She must've been really tired today. Miriam never goes to bed this early." Robert said, walking back into the kitchen. "I don't blame her...she didn't sleep that well last night."

"Oh poor thing." Mary said, cleaning the dishes in the sink. "I hope she rests well tonight."

"She probably will." Robert said, walking over before leaning against the counter. "So...what do you want to do?"

Mary continued to wash the dishes before she stopped, soon looking at him. "What do you mean?"

"Well I mean...Miriam is in bed early. Do you want to go out for a walk?" Robert replied, looking at her and waiting to hear an answer.

She looked at him before looking down at the dishes, thinking about his offer before setting the plates down. "I would enjoy that."

He smiled brightly before he walked out of the kitchen, planning on getting his jacket.

It didn't take long before the two were on an adventure, walking around the county in the early evening. The sky was an vibrant orange, the sun easing itself behind the hills.

"Wow...that's a beautiful sunset." Robert said softly, looking at it.

"It sure is." Mary said quietly, looking at it before she looked at Robert. With the two of them having grown closer, she soon started to think more in regards of making their relationship a bit more than friends. "Can I show you something?"

Robert heard her, turning his head and looking at her before he smiled softly. "Yeah of course."

Mary smiled brightly before leading him into the woods, walking in a certain direction. As for Robert, he wasn't sure where she was taking him, which made him a little nervous. Eventually, the two arrived in a rather large open area in the woods, a grass area that was decorated with wildflowers.

"Wow..." Robert quietly said to himself, stepping forward and starting to walk towards the flowers. "They're beautiful."

Mary stood behind Robert, watching his response before walking with him again. "I know. I love coming to this place. It reminds me of so many happy memories." She said before she began to lay down in the grass, looking at the sky that had become as orange as a Doris Longwing Butterfly's wing.

Robert watched what she did before he followed her actions, lying next to her as the two watched the sky. "You have quite the spot...especially one that you value." He smiled softly, relaxing on the grass.

The two watched the sky for a few, enjoying the time to relax with each other. Eventually, Robert spoke up, a question that had been resonating within him.

"How come you didn't want to let us live with you a few months ago?" He quietly said, still looking at the sky, some clouds gently moving along in the sky.

Mary heard him and gave him a confused look. "What do you mean?"

"You were talking to Bishop David the morning after the rainstorm. You told him that you didn't want anyone staying at the house because you didn't have enough food and didn't want housing people. Part of me though doesn't believe that."

Mary listened to what Robert was saying, her expression staying confused before her expression became more of a look of hesitant.

"There's something more than not enough food and not wanting to house people huh? You don't have to tell me, but just know I'm here if you want to talk." Robert said quietly, wanting to assure that she could trust him.

She listened to what he said before she began biting her own lip, thinking to herself before she let out a quiet sigh. "There is...there's a lot more to it. I think it's fair that you should know."

He heard her response to his question and turned onto his side, looking at her now as she began to speak about what the reason for not wanting anyone to live with her.

"It all has to do with a man I loved...a man named William." Mary said quietly.

Chapter VI

William Bradshire...a carpenter of Lancaster County. Most of the county knew him as the kind man who cared about everyone around him, even the ones who didn't care for him. William was the prime example of what it means to follow Christ's footsteps. He showed a strong love towards God, helped out around his community, showed love towards everyone, taught the youth about the Bible, and that's just the peak of the iceberg.

Sometimes in life though, bad things can occur that change one's life. For William, it was losing his parents at the age of eighteen. With his parents gone, he now owned the house, but that meant nothing to William. For a long time, he had struggled with the fact that his parents were gone, but during this time, he still continued to help people, having put them first before himself.

A great example of William putting others first was one cold, dark night. There was a knock on his door, the knock having echoed the entire silent household. When William opened his front door, he found a shivering girl his age, looking up at him. This girl was Mary.

The young girl had ran away from home, angry at her parents and her peers around her community. She was looking for a place to stay, which was she ended up on William's doorstep, a stranger to him. William was caring enough to immediately let her in; he even allowed her to stay as long as she needed. Even though she could've left any time, she found herself a priceless friendship.

Eventually, as time progressed, the redhead soon fell in love with William, the same happening with the boy. The two ended up revealing their love for each other when they discovered and rested in the grass area in the woods with the wildflowers. Ever since then, they were two peas in a pod.

As time progressed, they became closer and closer, almost being one soul. Mary began helping out in the community with him while developing a strong love of God since William introduced her to Him. Eventually, William decided that he was going to ask Mary for her hand in marriage, but his colleagues asked for his help in finishing the construction of a barn.

Unfortunately, William never had the chance to pop the question due to the accident. While he was watching his colleagues raise one of the barn walls up by pulling it up with ropes, the ropes snapped and the wall soon fell on William, his chances of escaping the wall very low with how fast the whole situation took. Sadly, William didn't survive the heavy barn wall crushing him.

Word soon got out around the county about William dying from the accident, which Mary soon heard about. She was devastated, crushed, her heart torn into pieces for the loss of her one true love.

After William had passed, Mary was given the house, considering she basically lived there and was a member of the community. During this time, Mary closed herself off from the rest of the world, locking herself away in her home, mourning the loss of William. She even decided to not let anyone into the house after the loss in order to keep the house peaceful, like it was when William and her were in it.

Even in the present, Mary still has nightmares about the whole incident, nightmares that remind her of the loss of William.

"If only I were there to stop him...to get him out of the way...If only I were there...he'd still be alive."

Chapter VII

Once Mary finished telling Robert the story, she had developed some tears from the memory of William's death.

"Now you know why I don't let anyone into the house...I know...it sounds insane, for the girlfriend of someone who has departed to keep the house like a temple. You must think I'm crazy..." Mary said quietly, wiping her tears.

"Oh no..." Robert said, looking at her. "I don't think you're insane at all...I can see why you value the house so much. All the memories with William...the laughter...the peace...everything about it...you don't want anyone to ruin this place for you." He said softly, gently resting his hand on hers. "I'm sorry...I didn't know this was the reason why you didn't want us here."

Mary heard him and finally broke down, tears rolling down her cheeks as she covered her face with her hands, muffled crying heard behind it. Robert reached for her and wrapped his arms around her, holding her close as he embraced her.

"Shhh...it's okay...Mary." Robert quietly said, stroking her hair gently to calm her down. "It's okay..."

After years of suppressing the memories of William and her, the pain she has endured from remembering his death, the many tears she had held back, she finally broke down and let her tears flow.

"I miss him so much...every day I wish I could see him again...tell him that I wish I could've saved him from the wall...I wish I could've done something." She said, pressing her face against Robert's shoulder as she shook from her crying.

"You couldn't do anything Mary...you had no idea that would happen..." Robert said softly, continuing to hold her close as she cried against him. "Look on the bright side...with William having a strong love for God, he's finally in Heaven where he can be with God...walk along with him...talk to him...laugh with him."

With Robert's words entering Mary's ears, it made her cry more. He was right in the sense that she wouldn't have known and that he's in a better place now. Her heart ached as she recalled all the memories of William from when they met to his death. All the memories were mainly happy and ones that would make her laugh whenever she looked back to them. Even though William was gone, she remembered one thing...William lives on through her. The memories, the house, the ideology, everything that William was made up of lives on through Mary. With this thought, she felt like she could finally get over the tragedy of losing William and achieve peace.

"Thank you...Robert...Thank you." Mary said quietly, looking up at him with tears in her eyes.

Robert looked down at her, confused as to why she was telling him thank you. "For what?" He laughed gently, wiping the tears away from her eyes.

"For saying all of those things about William and I...I've spent all these years holding onto William's tragedy and blaming myself for not being able to help him, but now I can finally find peace and let go of the tragedy...thank you...Robert." She finally said, looking at him as she gently reached up, stroking his cheek before she finally decided to lean in, kissing him gently.

Robert was caught off guard with the kiss, his eyebrows raising as she held her in his arms. Eventually, she broke the kiss, resting her head on his should. "Let's go back home...it's getting late." Mary said quietly, her eyes now closed.

Even though Robert had thought about pushing their relationship to another level, there was something that was holding him from reaching that level, something that had followed him from his previous home.

Chapter VIII

Many weeks had passed by since Mary told Robert about her past. Mary was in a much brighter mood, slowly building herself up again by socializing with people, going to church again, which made Bishop David happy, and she started wearing colorful clothes again.

Robert was thinking about what Mary had done in the wildflower area in the woods on the porch. He wanted to moved towards the next step, but the past was catching up with him.

"Hey!" Mary called out, coming up to the house with Miriam. "We've got dinner!"

He snapped back into reality, smiling gently when he saw the two. "Oh...that's wonderful. Looks delicious." Robert said, standing up and helping them take the food inside the house.

"I decided to cook something special for you...to thank you for helping me return back to my old self again."

Robert smiled and chuckled nervously, rubbing the back of his neck. "Oh...you don't have to do that."

"But papa," Miriam spoke out, looking at him, "look at the food! It looks delicious! At least let mom...Mary cook it for me."

Both Robert and Mary laughed at Miriam's comment, Mary picking her up and holding her.

"Okay, well if Robert doesn't want his special dinner, then I'll cook it for you." She said, walking in with the child.

"That'd be fantastic!" Miriam exclaimed happily.

Robert followed behind the two with the groceries, his expression being lost in thought as he thought about the past.

———

Dinner time soon arrived, everyone now seated at the table as they waited for Mary to come in with the special dinner.

"Whatever she's cooking, it smells delicious." Miriam said, excited to eat.

In a matter of minutes, Mary came out with a cooked turkey, the skin being a golden crisp.

Even though Robert wasn't asking for a special dinner, he was impressed with how the turkey came out. "Wow, looks really good Mary."

She smiled brightly, setting the plate down. "Well I'm glad you like it so much. I've got more coming out. I cooked some corn, made so mashed potatoes, have some greens." Mary explained to them as she walked back into the kitchen.

It took a few trips for her before she finally could sit down at the table with the two. "Alright, dig in." Mary said, taking her knife and fork, cutting into the turkey and scooping up a little bit of everything.

The dinner that they had all together was nice. Lots of laughter, lots of compliments, complete joy filled the room between Miriam and Mary, although Robert was most of the time quiet. After dinner, Miriam decided to go play with her doll in the living room while Mary and Robert were in the kitchen, cleaning the dishes.

While they were in there, Robert remained quiet, lost in his thoughts as he kept trying to shake it off. It didn't take too long though for Mary to see something was bothering him.

"You've been awfully quiet this evening...is there something wrong?" Mary asked him, continuing to wash the dishes.

"No." Robert said vaguely, not wanting to get into what was bothering him.

"You sure?" She said softly, looking at him. "You seem like you're thinking really hard about something."

"Don't worry about it." Robert said to her, trying to avoid explaining his thoughts.

Eventually, Mary let out a quiet sigh before setting her dish down, turning toward Robert.

"You know if something is troubling you, you can te-" Mary began to say to him.

"Drop it." Robert said harshly, looking at her for a few quick seconds before he finally set his plate down, shaking his head. "Just forget it...I'm going to bed." He said, leaving the kitchen and walking upstairs.

Mary was shocked by the way Robert reacted, considering it wasn't normal for Robert to be this way.

Miriam heard the commotion from the living room, looking at Mary. "Is papa upset about something?" She said with a concerned voice.

Mary heard Miriam and shook her head. "Don't worry about it dear. He just needs some time to himself."

Chapter IX

Robert currently laid in Mary's bed upstairs, his eyes closed as he tried sleeping. He didn't mean to snap at Mary, but considering his thoughts were getting to him, it was bound to happen. As he attempted to sleep, he soon felt something lay next to him, which interrupted his slumber.

He opened his eyes and turned to look and see if it was Mary.

Of course, he was right in this situation. Mary was in her nightgown, having crawled in bed with Robert, getting cozy. Once he saw it was Mary, he returned back to his previous position, his back facing her. Still trying to avoid breaking the news to Mary, he soon felt her arms around his stomach, her body soon pressing against his back.

"What's going on with you? You're usually not like this." She said softly, resting her head against his back.

"I don't know Mary...I don't know." Robert said quietly, his eyes still closed.

"I feel like you do know Robert." Mary finally said. "I just feel like you don't want to tell me what you're thinking of."

He heard what she said, but didn't reply to it. The only thing he did was sit in silence with his eyes closed, trying to fall into slumber.

"You know I'm here if you want to tell me what's bothering you. I think it'd be healthy if you did though because you won't get any sleep with you thinking about whatever you're thinking. I know from experience." Mary quietly said, now closing her eyes as she rested her head against his back.

Robert listened to what she was saying before he let out a quiet sigh, trying to think about how he would explain his thoughts to her. Eventually, he decided to be straightforward with her.

"You know why I decided to move to Lancaster County?" He asked Mary quietly.

She merely shook her head against his back, indicating that she didn't know why he moved here. "Aside from finding a new home, no I don't."

Robert listened to what she had to say before he continued. "I left my previous home because my wife walked out on Miriam and I."

When Mary heard this, her eyes opened up and she sat up, looking down at him. "What? That's horrible! Why would she do that?"

Once Mary sat up, Robert turned so that he was laying on his back, now looking up at her. "To be honest...maybe I married the wrong person. She just...everything seemed fine to me. She was a good mother, I was a good father, we lived a happy life, but then one day…" He said before stopping, thinking back to that day before telling Mary what happened.

"Sara?" He called out, looking around his home. "Where are you?

While he walked around the house, Miriam watched him, not understanding what was going on. "Papa? What's going on?"

"I can't find mom. She's gone." Robert said, his tone being a little more scared. "Maybe she left something saying where she went. Yeah…she leaves notes."

"Maybe…I'll help you try and find something" Miriam said, getting off of the couch before walking around their home, trying find anything that could lead to the mystery of where Robert's wife went.

Eventually, Miriam found a note that had fallen on the side of the bed. "Papa!" She called out. "I found a note!"

Robert immediately ran into the room, seeing the note in Miriam's hand. He took the note from her and began reading it. Although the hope he had on his expression when he found the note soon faded the more he continued to read it. In fact, he soon had become emotionless from what was written on the note.

"What does it say papa?" Miriam asked, looking up at him.

Robert finished reading the note, looking down at Miriam before folding the note in half, tucking it into his pocket. "Don't worry about it sweetheart. I think though...we need to move away from this county."

When Miriam heard this, she was completely confused. "Why? Why do we need to move?"

He heard her before he picked her up, looking around the house one last time. "Because I think we will find somewhere else that'll be better for the both of us."

"We basically left the county with nothing but the clothes on our back. I couldn't stand living in the same county as her and live in a house that we lived in together." Robert said quietly, looking at Mary as he finished explaining his story. "Would you stay in the same place if you found out your love left you and your child for someone else?"

When Mary heard this, she let out a depressed sigh. "No...I don't think I would." She said quietly. "Is that what's been on your mind today?"

Robert heard her before nodding softly. "I've been thinking about it for a long time now...I've wanted to move onto the next step in our relationship, but...I fear that something would happen again...I fear the odds of you walking out on us."

Once Robert said that, Mary spoke up in a more serious tone. "Robert...look at me."

Robert did as told and look into her eyes, seeing what she would say.

"I would never do that...ever in my life." Mary said, looking at him as she gently rested her hand on his cheek. "I wouldn't do something to hurt you and Miriam...I love you both, with all my heart." She said to him before she gently kissed him, breaking it soon after before resting her head on his chest. "You don't need to worry about me every walking out on you two...I care about you two so much that my heart aches. I wouldn't even think about walking out on you two."

When Robert heard this, he let out a relieved sigh, his arms wrapping around her and hugging her against him. "I love you so much Mary..."

"I love you too Robert..."

THE END

LOVE UNLIKELY

LOVINA SWANSON

Chapter 1

Haylee lay in the darkness of her room staring out of the window at the moon that hung low in the sky, her only consort in her lonely life of misery and depravity. Four years after meeting Jase her heart was broken into a million pieces and scattered across the vast expanse of her own insignificant universe. Move on, they said, he's not worth it, they said, you deserve better. What did they know? None of her so called friends could ever imagine how she felt deep down and how utterly destroyed she was when she walked in on Jase in the arms of her best friend, Lucile. Of course the first thing both of them shouted when caught in the act was – it's not what you think! – The most default response.

After Jase pleaded with her and Lucile convinced her that it was an irresponsible judgement error on her part and that it would never happen again, she gave it another shot. She should have known better. Naïve little Haylee, who only tries to see the good in people ended up as the biggest fool of them all and when it happened a second time, she could no longer be ignorant. It was obvious that between the chemical combination of Lucile's raging pheromones and Jase's ego boosted testosterone, she never stood a chance. She had to finally admit to herself that she was never going to find true love, and friendships are feeble pastimes for pre-schoolers.

It's been almost two months since her relationship with Jase ended, and it wasn't long after that, that she also handed in her resignation as an article clerk. Breaking up with Jase and seeing him once in a blue moon she could handle well, but working with him and sharing the same open office day in and day out was a little too much to handle. It amazed her how men in particular, could be so callous and move on without a worry in the world. She had managed thus far, but the more she sat at home she started to feel cooped up like a bird in a too small cage.

She sighed and tugged her blanket over her shoulders and tucked it under her chin as she turned unto her other side, this time staring at her graduation photo. She stood tall and proud, alone in her toga with her rolled up certificate in her hand, no immediate family to share her successes with her. Her mother, or rather adoptive mother had passed away six months short of her graduation that year. Haylee sniffed and blinked away the tears. She didn't cry then and she won't cry now. Finally giving up on sleeping she tossed the blanket back and sat up in bed. Her mom always told her, that every person has left something behind in their past, that sits there and waits until they go back to find it and resolve it. And until recently she had never thought she wanted to go back there. She was only four when she was adopted, a lonely grey mouse stuck in foster care. From the first day she arrived at her new family, she was accepted and spoiled rotten. She never needed for anything in her life, and she never felt as if she was any different to any of the other kids, so why she suddenly felt like digging out the past was a mystery to her, but every day it became more and more pressing. And here at two in the morning, she was stuck between forcing herself to sleep or logging into her email to see if the adoption agency managed to track down her biological mother or family. Insomnia won the battle and she finally made herself a cup of coffee and sat down at her desk and logged into her emails.

Dear Miss Jones

We have managed to track down your biological mother, but it is with regret that we inform you that she passed away a few years ago due to illness. We have however managed to track down her parents, your grandparents. We do however wish that you consider the fact that they may not...

Hayley stared at the email, reading it over and over again, somehow grief evaded her, and it was like reading the sad story of a stranger. What she did learn from this was that her mother was born Amish, and that her grandparents lived in an Amish community in Ethridge,

Tennessee. But even if she knew who they were, what good would that do now? It wasn't as if she could reunite with her long lost mother anymore. But what she might be able to figure out is what type of woman her mother was and what type of life she lived. Maybe it will even shed some light on why her mother gave her up for adoption. As she spent her time reading up on the Amish and their culture, it became more and more evident that her mother may not have had a choice, but this was pure speculation. And unless she took the time to find these things out for herself, she would always be guessing about the woman who brought her into this world.

Besides, it wasn't as if she had anything better to do with her time. She had no job, no love life and no coffee, she thought as she looked at the empty canister in front of her.

That was it; she was going to take the last of her savings and head to Ethridge and find the Lapp's.

Chapter 2

The whole way to Ethridge, Hayley kept wondering if she was making a mistake. She was about to embark on a journey she was in the least bit prepared for. Before she left everything behind, she made effort to reinvent her wardrobe with a few modest outfits just so that she wouldn't look too outrageous amongst the Amish. But even now as she sat in the back of the cab, her heart was beating a million miles a second and she was on the verge of having a nervous breakdown. She had just left behind the only life she knew, not that there was much left of her for her to salvage, but she was somewhat comfortable where she was.

The cab pulled into the small town of Ethridge and stopped in front of what appeared to be a touring business.

"This is as far as I can go missy," the cab driver said and pointed to this meter.

Hayley nodded and fished for cash to pay the cab driver and the moment her bags were offloaded and she stood like a singled out deer in hunting season outside on the sidewalk she wanted to burst out in tears. Whatever was she thinking coming out here?

"Hello, may I help you?"

Startled Hayley nearly lost her balance as she spun to look at the stranger behind her, "Oh-I-um, well, I'm looking for someone," she said and dug in her purse, "Mr and Mrs Lapp?"

"Oh Fredrick and Mary Lapp, yah, they live here. I can take you," the young man said.

"You know them?" Hayley asked in disbelief.

"Yah, well it's a small community we all know each other," he said tucking his thumbs under his suspenders.

Hayley couldn't help but stare, wondering if all Amish men were this good looking. This guy couldn't be much older than her twenty five. And although he was dressed modestly in what she had to assume

Amish clothes, he looked reasonably attractive. She was never one for men with hairy faces, but for some reason his beard which was slightly trimmed suited him perfectly. He had ebony black hair with willow green eyes set deeply in his skull.

"If you're done staring..." he said interrupting her thoughts with his brows drawn together.

Embarrassingly she shook her head, "I'm so sorry, I just... it has been a really long day and I've travelled a long way."

"No matter, my name is Duncan," he said and nodded his head courteously, extending his hand.

"Hayley," she said and gave his hand an overly firm shake.

"Well I best be getting you to the Lapp's, the weather is turning foul."

Without notice he started loading her luggage into a carriage that stood nearby and then patted the back of the carriage, indicating her seat.

Who was she to ask questions, she hadn't the foggiest about their customs and every website she visited to learn about them were know-it-all windbags who have made up assumptions. So instead of opposing she hopped into the back of the carriage and sat down.

"So do you know the Lapps?" Duncan called over his shoulder as they made their way into the town.

"I...sort of, actually, I knew their daughter," she lied, she had no clue what their daughter was like. Just because Hannah Lapp gave birth to her, didn't exactly mean she knew her.

"I think you might have them mistaken for someone different, they only have a son, but Kendrick moved to Lancaster with his wife."

Well this was a good start, she thought as she tucked her lip under her teeth, "Perhaps I am confused, but I suppose there is no harm in meeting them. Maybe they might know Hannah Lapp as extended family."

"Hannah Lapp," Duncan repeated, "The name sounds familiar."

The carriage came to a halt and Hayley fell forward along with her luggage and just then the heavens opened up.

"Come!" Duncan called and reached for a sheet to cover her luggage before effortlessly lifting her off the wagon and placing her on her feet, "The Lapp's live here, if you hurry I can wait and take you back to Richland Inn."

"Wait, what do you mean back to town, I need to be here in Ethridge," she protested as Duncan lead her up to the house where the Lapps lived.

"Well if the Lapps won't let you stay in their home, you have nowhere else to stay, unless you want to sleep in the barn."

"The barn?" she asked appalled.

"Duncan, vas in der velt?" an elderly man interrupted as he opened his door.

Duncan immediately removed his hat and clutched it in front of him then looked at her before turning his attention back to the older man.

"Mister Lapp, this is Hayley. She's come to Ethridge to look for..."

Before Duncan could continue Hayley stepped up and extended her hand, "Grandfather?"

The older man's complexion paled, and he exchanged looks with Duncan then looked at Hayley, "You're mistaken," he mumbled and moved to close the door, but then an elderly woman appeared and the expression on her face was one of pure shock.

"Hannah... you look just like her," she said in a trembling voice as her eyes shot full of tears.

"Grandmother?" Haylee said as she stood with her hands folded in front of her.

"Come dear child, you're going to get soaking wet out in the rain," she said as she dragged Hayley into the house, despite her Grandfather's disapproval.

And as she disappeared into the kitchen she heard her grandfather mumble for Duncan to bring her luggage inside.

Her grandparents, she couldn't believe it. She was actually in the very house her biological mother grew up in. Her grandmother seemed far more accepting of her than her grandfather did, but she refused to make any assumptions until she had all the facts. For now she will take the time she had to get to know them.

Chapter 3

A week since her arrival and all she could determine was that her mother, Hanna Lapp went on a Rumspringa and never returned.

"Did she never write to you?" Hayley asked her grandmother one morning after her grandfather left to go to work.

"She wrote to us, but only ever to let us know she was fine," her grandmother said softly as she continued with her sewing.

"But weren't you in the least bit worried?"

Mary put down her sewing and reached out for Hayley's hand, "Yah, we were worried, especially your grandfather, but our laws are different to those on the outside. Hannah made her choice and she had a chance to return."

Hayley sat quietly for a moment and squeezed her grandmother's hand. The short while she had been here in the Amish community of Ethridge, she had found a sense of peace and tranquillity she never felt before. With the exception of a minority of locals who walked wide circles around her, the younger people like her were friendly and very accommodating. She couldn't understand why her mother would have left for good, and trade this life for what lay outside in the world. But then, being on holiday in a strange place was far different that living the life in full.

A knock on the door drew her attention and her grandmother quickly set her sewing aside and went to open the door, and a few seconds later she returned with Duncan in tow.

"Hayley, Duncan is here to see you," her grandmother said smiling.

Duncan was another person she was growing fond of at an alarming rate, but thankfully the walls she erected around herself kept her level headed. She knew that the only reason she felt closer to him than any of the others was because he was the first person she met when she arrived.

"Hi Duncan, what a nice surprise," she said standing up.

"Good day to you Hayley," he nodded tucking his thumbs in his suspenders, "I was wondering if you would like to go to the market today, I have a few errands to run."

Hayley felt the slight flutter of butterflies in her stomach and tugged her hand into her midriff. It would be rather nice to get out a little and get to know other parts of the community, she thought and then nodded.

"It would be lovely, let me get my coat and purse," she said and hurried to her room.

She forced herself not to eavesdrop on her grandmother' and Duncan's conversation and quickly got what she needed before joining them.

In no time they were on the carriage and on their way to the market, this time Hayley got to sit in the front and not like some baggage on the back.

"So how are you enjoying your stay here in Ethridge?" Duncan asked curiously.

"It's nice. I mean, it's very different to city life, but so far I'm enjoying the peace and quiet," she said and glanced out over the landscape.

"Yah, it's very quiet. So did you manage to find out about Hannah?"

"A little," she said, but decided not to elaborate. She didn't want to put the Lapps in any sort of disrepute, but she found it hard to believe that Duncan had no clue about her, but then again, he was probably still a baby when Hannah left the Amish community.

"So will you be moving on then?" he said clearing his throat.

Hayley turned to look at him and smiled, "Not sure, maybe. Tell me about this Rumspringa thing."

Duncan laughed and looked at her, "Well, Rumspringa means to run around, when the youngsters turn sixteen they can choose to go out and experience things outside of our community. It's each one's choice, some do it and some don't."

"Did you ever, I mean did you do it when you turned sixteen?" she asked curiously.

"Nay, I never did. I have all I need right here."

"So you never wonder what lies out in the cities."

Duncan drew the carriage to a halt and then turned to look at Hayley, studying her with those intense willow green eyes.

"Most young men leave because they are not satisfied with their life here, mostly because they are tempted by the modern world, and women," he said and for some reason his cheeks grew rosy.

Hayley tried to hide her smile and coughed softly, "So you never wanted to go find some hanky-panky?"

"Hanky -panky?" Duncan asked and blinked, "What is that?"

"Uh... well meeting women, dating and so on."

Duncan threw his head back and laughed, "Oh no, I had no interest in those things. Not then anyway," he said and then tugged on the reins sending the horse back unto the road, "I always believed that at the right time God will send the right woman my way. I'm a patient man Hayley Jones."

When he looked at her then, she felt her heart flutter in her chest and she immediately looked the other way. Her mind was clearly playing tricks on her; there was no way that Duncan would even consider looking at her twice. She was an outsider for one, and secondly she wasn't exactly a virgin either. And although she still knew very little about their laws and traditions, she was sure the Amish probably had the highest moral values in the world second to nuns.

The rest of their trip was in silence, and a few miles further they finally reached the Amish Country Mall. Hayley was quite surprised by the variety of goods that were sold at this place, but more so how many non-Amish visited the place. It was like a tourist distraction for curious people. And as she stood next to Duncan and the Carriage in her own authentic Amish dress, a sense of pride washed over her. Surprised that she actually felt Amish in some farfetched way, she smiled at Duncan and then headed into the shop. She found it quite amusing that it was called a Mall when all it really had were old antique trinkets and a limited menu of food. There were some items for sale but it was hardly considered anything close to a shopping Mall. She did her bit to get a few items for herself and when she next exited, she found Duncan standing next to her grandfather, both in deep conversation. Instead of barging in on them she took a walk around the store to give them their own time. Her grandfather had hardly spoken a word to her since her arrival and he was still a great big mystery to her. On occasion when she did ask her gran about him, she simply avoided the topic. She wasn't any closer to find out exactly why her mother never came back.

Chapter 4

Duncan couldn't help but admire Hayley, and although she was an outsider, she seemed to adapt quite well to the Amish life. It's been two weeks since he met her, and the more time he spent with her the more he started to like her. The first day he saw her was the first time he ever really looked at a woman. She was modestly dressed in a floral print dress that flowed elegantly down her body to her calves, but what intrigued him most was her shyness. The fact that he had the impulsive need to run his fingers through her long brown tresses was abnormal for him and he quickly stifled that need, by reminding himself that she was an outsider, which helped.

Normally when outsiders visited the Amish communities they stuck to their modern clothes, where the women wore as little as possible. No wonder so many of the Amish boys opted to go on their expedition to the cities, being tempted by the promises that the modern world presented. Two of his own best friends went out to experience the world and all it had to offer, but he never felt that desire or pull to know what happens out there. He was more than content to live this life of simplicity, working on the farm and making goat's cheese. There were many times when he attended the sings and where he contemplated the option of taking a wife, but none of the girls here in Ethridge ever made him feel the way he did now. And he was adamant that if he was going to take a wife, it would be someone who would completely consume his thoughts. He wanted the same love with a wife than his mother and father shared. He had never seen them argue, and they always showed their affection towards each other. And if they could have such a devoted marriage, why could he not have the same?

Duncan was caught in his own thoughts when the smell of burning wood and grass wafted through the air.

"Duncan!" It was Hayley who rode towards him on one of the Lapp's horses, her eyes wide, "Come quick, my grandfather's barn is on fire!" she cried.

In an instant Duncan had called his father and his neighbours, and everyone else he could alert and they were on their way by carriage to the Lapp's farmlands. Up ahead he could see the plume of fire explode into the grey sky. Flames rolled outwards and embers were flying up into the sky.

When he pulled up next to Hayley where she dismounted the horse, he took the reins and handed it to another young man, "Take the horse to my father's barn and keep it there," he instructed and then turned to Hayley, "What happened?"

"I have no idea, we were all having dinner when we heard the loud crash of lightning, and not long after that the smoke was everywhere," she said ringing her hands together.

Duncan's concern for Hayley had to be set aside, and although he wanted to comfort her, he had to attend to the bigger problem.

"Okay, go to the house and stay inside," he ordered as he scooped a bucket of water from the trough.

"But I can help," she protested and reached for a small barrel.

"You've done enough, now go and sit with your grandmother, I'm sure she could use the company."

Her mouth opened in protest but then shut, and with a slight nod, she ran across the field towards the house.

They fought all night to get the fire under control, thankfully the Lord had blessed them with rain to help put the fire out, but all that was left were the charred remains of the barn in the smoky morning air that reeked of burnt wood and straw. His father had warned Fredrick about the tall dead tree that stood so close to the barn. But misfortune led to lighting striking the dead tree and causing it to fall on to the barn. Luckily it was only the barn that burned down, somehow the horses were freed before the barn was completely on fire, and he has the slightest suspicion that it was Hayley's quick thinking that saved the animals. As for the equipment, it was all replaceable.

"Thank you son, if you didn't arrive when you did I would have lost all my horses," Mr Lapp said as he came to stand next to Duncan.

"Nay, that was not my doing. Hayley saved the horses," he said and looked at the older man.

"Hayley saved them?" he asked disbelievingly.

"Yah, she came to fetch me on horseback, I've never seen a woman ride so well, but she came to call me straight away. By the time I got here the horses were already in the fields and Kent took them to my barn."

Fredrick stood quietly for a while rubbing his beard, and Duncan knew that he had his own demons to face. He too had never heard of Hannah Lapp, but spending time with Hayley he had learned a great deal.

"She's seeking your approval," Duncan said crossing his arms as both of them looked at what remained of the barn, "She deserves a fair chance."

"You're right," Fredrick said and then headed towards the house.

Duncan looked as the older man walked away, his shoulders hunched as if he carried a heavy burden, but he knew Hayley deserved a fair chance, she had nothing to do with her mother's disobedience or her choice to give her up for adoption.

Later that day, Duncan stood in his father's barn, grooming the Lapps' horses. The least he could do was make sure that none of them were injured. But more than anything he needed to keep busy so that he could chase the thoughts of Hayley from his mind. Every waking hour was seemingly consumed by thoughts of her, and after her courageous act it was even worse. Now he knew exactly how King Solomon must have felt, being tempted by a beautiful woman.

"Duncan?" he heard Hayley's voice from outside the barn.

"In here!" he answered and tossed the brush in the sack hanging on the wall.

"Oh there you are," she said smiling and held out a basket for him, "Grandma and I baked these to thank you for helping us out with the horses."

Duncan smiled and took the basket filled with cookies, "Thanks, but I think you deserve all the credit, if it wasn't for you these horses would be charred with the barn."

He noticed Hayley blush as she averted her eyes, "I love horses, I had to do something."

Duncan stepped closer and reached out to tuck his finger under her chin, "And you did an amazing job of saving them," he said but his voice betrayed him.

This close to her, he could smell the fresh scent of lavender and vanilla, and although it was just the crook of his finger brushing her unblemished skin under her chin, it was the silk soft smoothness that tempted him more than anything. And without a second thought he stepped in and pressed his lips against hers. Hers were soft, like cotton pillows and although the kiss was brief, it was a defying moment for him. He knew there and then that Hayley was the woman he'd been waiting for all these years.

He broke the chaste kiss but didn't step away from her; instead he kept his eyes locked on hers. It was that moment between two people where words were irrelevant syllables and consonants were fleeting sounds that would never be able to express the emotions that sparked between them.

It was Hayley that stepped away first, and how shyly tucked a strand of hair behind her ear.

"My grandfather said that they will be doing a barn rising this coming weekend, will you come?" she asked softly.

"I wouldn't miss it for the world," Duncan said.

And as Hayley walked back out of the Barn she looked back over at him again and smiled.

Duncan felt like a teenager for the first time, and now more than ever was he determined to make Hayley Jones his wife.

Chapter 5

The barn raising was well on its way, the men from the community had spent most of the morning working and Hayley was amazed by how quickly the barn started taking shape. She heard many stories about this experience and how the Amish are able to build an entire barn in one day, but she had never seen it with her own eyes. Duncan was at the front line of everything. He did the planning and the design, his skill as a builder came in handy and it appeared that young to old admired him, but not nearly as much as she did.

When she first decided to come to Ethridge, finding love was the last thing she anticipated. After her failed engagement to Jase, she had sworn off on ever dating again, but here she was, utterly captivated by Duncan. He was the complete opposite to Jase. He was kind, considerate, a true gentleman and there was something about him that she craved.

"He's a fine young man," her gran said as she handed her the basket of fresh fruit.

Hayley tore her eyes away from the barn and smiled at her gran, "Yes, he is," she admitted.

"You know, Hannah never told us about you until after she gave you up for adoption," her grandmother started, "When she told us your grandfather begged her to withdraw the adoption and rather send you to us."

Hayley sat down opposite her gran at the wooden table, "So you did know about me?"

"Oh yes we did, but your mother had already handed you to your new parents, and we had no way of finding you. That day you arrived here in Ethridge, you were a splitting image of my Hannah."

Hayley's eyes shot full of tears and she reached out to take her grandmother's hand, "My adopted parents were good people, they really looked after me as if I was their own."

"I know, but I can't help wonder just how things would have been if Hannah had come back home," the older woman admitted and lowered her eyes.

"I'm here now though, and you've made me feel at home."

"Yah, yah, I know. I've been trying my best. Your grandfather blames himself for what happened, but he's a good man."

Hayley smiled and then looked back at the men toiling in the sun. Her grandfather was a proud but humble man, and she knew that deep down he cared for her.

By six o'clock that evening, the barn stood tall in all its glory. Brand spanking new as if no disaster had struck it just a week ago, and everyone in the community had gathered to celebrate the event. It was a festive atmosphere to say the least, and for the first time in her life Hayley felt as if she belonged. Over the weeks she spent here in Ethridge learning to bake and quilt, she hardly thought of her life in the city. And the hustle and bustle of peak hour traffic and busy shopping malls was nothing but a distant memory of a temporary life she once knew.

She made a few friends and even the older people had started to like her. Maybe it was due to the fact that she did not come here to dispute their faith or their ways, but she embraced it like any Amish citizen would.

From across the group of people she caught Duncan looking at her, but instead of looking away, she smiled at him, and even when one of his friends tapped him on his shoulder he still looked her way, refusing to drop his glance. She noticed immediately that he no longer had a beard, but that he had shaven, and the sight of him made her knees weak. It was she who first looked away when her grandfather came to sit beside her.

"My dear," he started sounding uncomfortable, "I owe you an apology for my behaviour."

Hayley turned to her grandfather and smiled, "No need, you had a lot to cope with, with my untimely arrival. I should have taken better care to notify you before I just dropped in."

"No, it's not that. I-I never gave your mother a chance to rectify things and for that I am forever guilty, I should have gone to find her."

Fredrick pinched the bridge of his nose and shut his eyes and Hayley knew he was fighting back the tears, she gently placed her hand on his, "The choices we make are our own, and we are all responsible for them, no one can take responsibility for the mistakes of others."

There was a moment of silence, and when her grandfather looked up at her again he smiled tenderly, "You will make a wonderful Amish woman," he said and patted her hand, "And Duncan would choose well to ask for your hand."

"Hayley, come!" One of the girls called and tugged her up by her hand, "You must join in on the sing."

Before Hayley could process the words of her grandfather she was caught smack bang in the middle with a bunch of the younger people, and although there were no instruments, the clapping of hands and the harmonies of voices made the songs come to life. Among the crowd was Duncan, subtly making his way closer to her and the closer he came the more her heart beat out of control and the butterflies that hijacked her insides fluttered up a storm. She might very well be an outsider but she could not deny the fact that somehow providence had claimed a victory.

"Would you spare me a few minutes of your time?" Duncan whispered as he reached her.

"Of course," she said and followed him outside.

Duncan had his hands tucked in his pockets as he stood outside. The moonlight spilled down from the heavens like a silver curtain, bathing their surroundings in silver dust and casting its subtle glow over them. And as Hayley came to stand next to him, they both glanced up into the sky.

"Hayley..."

"Duncan..."

They started at the same time and then burst out laughing.

"You first," Hayley insisted and Duncan smiled and turned towards her.

"Okay, well, I'm sure this will come as no surprise to you, but I thought it best I clear the air," he started clutching his hand in his hands, "I think or rather, I know that I have grown very fond of you, and I know that it may be a little more complicated than usual, but I have spoken to your grandfather."

Hayley stood playing with the string of her prayer cap, coiling it around her index finger nervously. It felt is if her heart was going to jump out of her throat as Duncan went on, explaining how he had asked her grandfather if he would allow him to court her. A few weeks ago, she would never have considered this, but now where she stood under the moonlit sky, with her hand in Duncan's she knew exactly what she wanted.

"And did my grandfather approve?" she asked curiously biting her lip.

"He did indeed, which is why I have gathered to courage to ask you in person," he admitted and smiled.

Hayley shifted her weight and sucked in a breath, she had no idea how Amish dating customs worked. Of all the things she had yet to learn, dating hardly featured and she recalled only briefly spot reading over that section.

"So are we going to be bundling?" she asked innocently and blushed.

Duncan raised his brows and chuckled, "My dear Hayley, you have so much to learn still, no one does that anymore," he said and stepped closer to her and reached to remove her prayer cap.

"Is that allowed?" She whispered softly as Duncan's lips hovered over hers and he pulled the pin that secured her hair in a bun lose.

"What happens between us, and the Lord, is all that matters," he said and then wrapped her lose braid around his hand and kissed her fully on the lips.

Chapter 6

Hayley stood in front of the mirror, while her grandmother fussed with her long hair. It's been a year since she joined the community and although her and Duncan's feelings for each other were no secret to the rest of the community, they both kept their word to follow the rules and customs as required by the Amish Council.

"So the food is almost ready. Once your Grandfather and I are off to the church service, you and Duncan can sit down and celebrate your betrothal."

Hayley looked in the reflection of the mirror at her grandmother, the woman she had grown to love and smiled, "Do you think I will make him happy, Grossmammi?" she asked.

"Natuurlijk! You're his future and the woman he had been waiting for all this time," her gran reassured her.

After her grandparents left to go to church, where the minister would be announcing the brides to be, she waited patiently at the house for Duncan to arrive. She kept looking at the clock on the wall, it was a unique hand crafted clock made especially for her by Duncan, as a courtship gift. Time however seemed like it had deliberately slowed down, and when she heard the carriage finally pull up in front of the house, she had to force herself to stay calm and not rush into his arms. Other than the first time he kissed her, and the second and the third, this was probably one of the most amazing moments in her life. After tonight, she would officially be engaged, and by October, only two months away, she would be Mrs. Hayley Beiler.

"You do know that you still have a choice right?" Duncan said much later, after they had finished dessert.

"I have made my choice, and it is to stay here with you," she said smiling.

They were seated on a wooden bench outside on the porch; waiting for the Lapp's to arrive.

"Are you a hundred percent sure?" he asked again, this time lacing his fingers with hers.

Hayley turned to him and placed her free hand over their entwined fingers. The past few months she had made the effort to learn their various customs, do bible study, get familiar with their laws, but she knew beyond anything that her life was here with him.

"Duncan, I am happy and I would not change this for anything," she said and then leaned close enough for her lips to brush his, "Ich liebe dich," she whispered and gave him a chaste kiss on his lips.

"And I love you, Hayley Jones," Duncan said, smiling from ear to ear and then quoted Songs of Solomon, "You are altogether beautiful, my darling, beautiful in every way."

~*~

Most of all, let love guide your way. Col 3:14

MAYBE AMISH

MEGAN MYERS

The storm had passed through the Indiana countryside leaving a trail of destruction that the rather large Amish community had not seen since many years ago, when Delilah was not even born yet. Back in those days, her mother, Miriam, was a very young woman of only twenty, and filled with hope for a bright and fulfilling future. It was Miriam's time to marry and start a family of her own according to Amish tradition, and she was in love with Abner. Abner was the son of Farmer Zeb Colvin, who farmed the acreage near Miriam's family farm. Ever since Miriam had been twelve years old, it was expected that she would marry Zeb's son, Abner, when they both came of marriageable age. Once the two reached nineteen, their courtship began, and a lovely traditional wedding had soon followed. Times were good then, for a while at least, as Miriam adjusted to married life. She kept house very well, and was a talented seamstress. She often crafted linens for the community because her sewing was of the finest quality. It was Miriam's God given gift to create beautiful bed covers, table clothes, baby clothing, and sometimes even wedding dresses for the Amish women of her village. Early married life seemed like a dream, as Miriam became pregnant with Deborah, the eldest girl child, followed swiftly by boppli Delilah. Then came Matthew, John, and James, all within fairly quick succession of one another. Miriam dreamed of having a big family, but the bopplis all came so swiftly, that life soon became stressful for the young couple. Abner worked in the pastures all day, while Miriam cared for the children, kept house, and had supper waiting on the table by the time Abner arrived home in the evening. Miriam and Abner began to have their differences given the demands of the farm, and the demands of keeping a tidy home. It was no easy task, given that Delilah's mother had had five little children under the age of seven running about the house. With Deborah being only seven, she was not equipped to help her mother manage the other siblings, plus attend school.

Within a year, Abner began to grow quite distant from his wife and children. It seemed that family life was not agreeable to Abner, and he spent more and more of his time working late into the night plowing the fields. When Abner did come home, once the children were fast asleep, he would demand his supper, and become irate if it was cold. Miriam could only keep up with so much, and she was fast learning that there was little hope of pleasing her unhappy husband. Arguments ensued night after night, and Deborah and her bruders could overhear much of the fighting between their parents. Delilah was still a dear little boppli, so was blissfully ignorant of the family discord. However, by the time Delilah had turned three years old, things had deteriorated even more so within the Colvin home. Abner was now becoming quite abusive to Miriam, accusing her of everything from bad housekeeping to terrible cooking. None of these things were factual, as Miriam worked hard to provide Abner with a happy family life. Abner was just plain hard to please, and turned out to be a very unhappy man. Whatever the reasons for Abner's ire and unhappiness, he began to do the unthinkable. He began to strike out at his harried wife at the end of the long days, eventually leaving her with many bruises. These marks she hid under her plain Amish clothing, and was sure to wear as many layers as possible as the abuse grew worse.

Soon, Miriam had more than just bruises to hide. Abner's temper became uncontrollable, and his wife ended up with a broken wrist. This further impeded her abilities to perform all the demands of family life in the household, which only fueled Abner's discontent. Miriam did not want to reveal what was going on in the home, because it was not the Amish way to hurt your wife. Miriam feared that she would be to blame, because after all, that is what Abner declared for much of their married life. After the broken wrist came more injuries, such as a several broken fingers, which rendered Miriam unable to sew. This then created more upset, since Miriam could not bring in extra money by sewing for the villagers. No one questioned Miriam's eventual halt in providing hand sewn goods, as they all believed she had too many bopplis to raise to be sewing in any of her spare time. This went on for many years, eventually crippling Miriam's once deft sewing fingers. It was enough just to keep a tidy home and cook the meals. Now that the maedel children were of age, they began to help their mamm with the daily chores and the cooking. Deborah eventually was forced to leave school early in order to help mamm manage the home. Delilah's time at school was quickly coming to a premature end as well, as Miriam bore yet two more bopplis in the span of three years. It was chaos to say the very least.

Time marched on for the Colvin clan, and Deborah was unhappy having to carry the burdensome chores mostly alone. Miriam was too exhausted and old before her time, thanks to an ungrateful and hateful Abner. Both maedels grew up believing that Abner's actions were the norm in all families. This of course, was not the case, but was the reality that the Colvin family experienced. Soon, Abner passed away from a sudden heart attack, leaving Miriam alone with the many children and the farm. It was now that Delilah's schwester, Deborah, was sixteen years old. The family was in dire straits despite the aid of the Amish community that tried their best to help for the poor widow and her children. The farm was too much for the young bruders to handle, as they were still of school age. Deborah found herself married at just sixteen years old to add an able male figure to the Colvin farm. She married Benjamin, who was but sixteen himself, far from ready to assume the duties of husband, but was thrust into the responsibilities nonetheless. Things improved little for the family, as Deborah seemed to follow in her mother's unfortunate footsteps by marrying a no good and cruel young man, who was not only lazy, but seemed much like Abner in temperament. Delilah could only watch on in horror, as history repeated itself within the home, with poor Deborah the present victim of Benjamin's constant temper tantrums and lazing about.

It was soon after Deborah's ill-fated marriage that Delilah felt she must speak up in defense of her schwester,

"Deborah, how long will you tolerate this behavior of Ben's? He treats you just like daed treated mamm all these years! Don't you long for something better?" said Delilah one morning.

"No, to tell you the honest truth, Delilah, I do not. Ben has his ways, but he's all this family has got anymore. We need Ben to provide.," answered Deborah. Delilah could scarcely believe what she was hearing, since her bruder-in-law was nothing but a brute and a man who could barely be bothered to do the plowing. Benjamin did the bare minimum as to not arouse suspicion from the other Amish men. They all believed that Benjamin was taking care of the large Colvin family as best he could. To be fair, the community had little clue or reason to believe otherwise that anything was amiss. Benjamin appeared jovial at services and gatherings, and Deborah was so accustomed to this way of life, having seen her own mother treated similarly all her life, that all seemed normal enough. It was not long before Deborah added to the many mouths to be fed. She gave birth to twins that summer. Delilah did her best to care for her younger siblings who were now also leaving school to help run the floundering farm. As young men, her bruders were expected to help at home, so their absence form school was not noticed to be out of the norm. It was already well known that the Colvin Farm was hard to keep up with so many children. Because Miriam was a widow, Deborah and Benjamin remained at the Colvin farm, living in an extension to the house that the Amish men built when they had married. It appeared to the community that Benjamin's presence was a positive force for the struggling family, so little thought was paid otherwise, as things began to worsen for Deborah. Benjamin did very little work in the fields, so the younger bruders soon picked up the slack. Delilah soon became jaded as to how men were supposed to behave, and vowed that she would never meet the same fate as her schwester and mamm.

As the years crawled by, Delilah found some escape in taking care of her small nephews. With Deborah out in the fields, Delilah changed the soiled windles of the twins, prepared appenditlich meals, and even took in a stray little Husky hundli. Delilah loved her nephews very much, and played with her hundli every chance she got. She named the hundli Jonny, and the dog soon became her only friend and confidante. Delilah would talk to her growing dog, and even sing hymns to him, as if he was one of the children of the family. She allowed Jonny to sleep in the old barn. Delilah saw the worst in the men in her life that were supposed to be responsible for her family's well-being. She came to trust no one, and resolved early on in her life that she preferred the life of an old maid over that of getting married to a man who would only mistreat her. She knew that not marrying within the Amish community was not unheard of, but certainly an uncommon event. Most Amish girls past the age of sixteen began the courtship ritual traditional within the faithful community, and would eventually marry and have families of their own. Delilah was not going to be part of this, and promised herself that somehow, she would survive on her own with her pup, Jonny by her side. It was very unfortunate that Delilah believed all men to be the same ilk as Abner and Benjamin. It was true that she saw kindness in her younger bruders as time went by, but she still was very wary of men in general. Almost all men in her Amish community were good and upright men of faith, and treated their wives and families very well, but Delilah never knew anything beyond what life had taught her.

There came that day after the worst storm in some time, that Delilah took on the task of traveling into the main Englisch town with some of the other Amish members to buy new supplies and sundries needed to rebuild and repair what damage the storm had reeked. While the young men went one way to the hardware store in town, the few maedels that went on the journey to town went to the little grocery on the other edge of town. Delilah, deciding that these village girls were more than capable of gathering the needed goods themselves, took a walk through the Englisch town. So much of it was foreign to her, as the Amish lived so simply and sparsely from the main folk of the town. She marveled at all the different shops selling so many kinds of things! There was a toy store with elaborate playthings she had never seen prior, and a quaint bakery nestled on the corner lot of Main Street. The bakery had a pretty chiseled sign declaring that it called The Cream Puff! She wondered what that must taste like as she had not even heard of such a thing. Across the street from the bakery was a beautiful old church with stained glass windows with an old wrought iron gate surrounding a lovely flower garden leading up to the church. Amish worshipped in one another's homes on a rotation basis, so this was yet another alien sight to Delilah. It was so mysterious and the stained glass so beautiful, that she decided to take a walk across the street and see if the church doors were open. As she approached the front garden, she heard come sort of commotion towards the back of the church, so she peeked behind some old oaks to see what she could see. As it happened, there she saw a little cabin away from the church along a little dirt path lined with wildflowers. There was a mama cat with her busslin playing in the small field adjacent to the church yard, and she heard the sounds of hammering coming from beyond the cabin. Thinking nothing of it, she returned to the front doors of the church, and peered inside. It was very pretty inside, with long pews and an alter at the front of the church where big bouquets of floral arrangements were set. Above the alter there hung a sturdy wooden cross, and to the left there was a small table that she slowly approached. Upon the table, there sat a stack of bibles. Delilah could smell the leather that encased each bible. There must have been fifty or so copies, and she was surprised to see so many opulent looking books in a church, for she was accustomed to the austere and simple life of the Amish. This simplicity was beautiful in its own way, though Delilah felt that the church must be a very nice environment to pray. With no one to observe her, Delilah sat down on the first pew, and began a silent prayer to Gott,

Dear Gott,

Please bless my family, and keep us safe from harm. Protect us from Benjamin's temper, and help us to be strong in the face of adversity. I trust that you have a plan for me, Gott, but I do not feel I quite belong in my community with the Amish. Is there another way, Gott? Please give me guidance, and bless Jonny too. Give me the strength of mind and body to know what's right in this confusing world, and do not let me fall into the same marriage with terrible men that my mamm and schwester have fallen into.

Amen.

Just as Delilah was finishing her silent plea to the Lord, she heard the side door of the little church open with a thud. As she looked up, away from the wooden cross where her eyes had been fixed in prayer, she saw a man standing there dressed in work clothes, and carrying a bucket and mop across to the other side of the church. He noticed her right away, as she was the only person in the church during the middle of the day, and he came closer,

"Hello, there. Did you come in to admire the stained glass?" the mysterious man asked.

"Why, yes, I suppose I did. I've never seen anything quite like such colorful windows before. It is lovely how the sunlight falls through the colors!' Delilah responded.

"Yes, I made those windows myself not too long ago. I'm glad to see the storm hasn't touched them. I'd hate to have to start over again. I can see from your simple dress that you are from the Amish? What brings you here to town," inquired the young man.

"We were hit mighty hard by the storm, and we needed to quickly replenish some of our supplies, so we came into town on the buggy," she replied, "Are you the caretaker of this church?"

"Yes, yes, that I am! My name is Duncan. My father took care of St. Mary's Church all his life, and when he passed away last winter, I decided to take on the work myself. The church doesn't really have anyone else willing to keep up the grounds, and clean up after services. I also care for the few cows and chickens that belong to the parish," said Duncan.

"That sounds like interesting work! I care for my nephews and help on my family's farm. My daed passed on too awhile back, so I help out best I can."

"You live alone with your family? A girl your age usually is married with kids of her own by the looks of you," said Duncan. Delilah thought that was rather presumptuous of him to say, although it was true enough. She was eighteen after all, and had avoided courtship thus far. He did not need to know why. No one needed to know why. All that mattered to Delilah was that she had already witnessed and experienced enough heartbreak for a lifetime, and that was not going to be the life for her.

"I must be going now," said Delilah, as she was sure she had spent too much time there anyway, but Duncan gently persisted,

"Delilah, I know that you are Amish, and that you worship God in your own unique way, but it's obvious you feel comfortable inside this church, even if it is to only admire the beauty of the stained-glass windows. You know that you are more than welcome to visit the church again if you feel like it. The minister keeps the doors open all the time. He believes the church should provide comfort to those who seek it, so he never locks those front doors. You don't have to come for Sunday service or anything like that. Anyway, I hope we'll see you around town again soon."

Delilah didn't give his words much thought at the time, and said a polite good bye. She returned to the buggy to meet the others, and off they went back to her own village.

Once Delilah was home again, and bustling around the farm doing chores, her mind inadvertently began to drift to memories of the church, and how she had prayed there and had felt so comfortable. She was surprised that she felt so comfortable in an Englisch church. Then there was the subject of the young man she had chanced to meet, Duncan. She allowed herself the tiny luxury of daydreaming while feeding the chickens...Duncan had been very muscular. He must work very hard around the church, because it was obvious that he cared a great deal about following in his father's footsteps. She thought that was an admirable thing for Duncan to want to do. The church yard had looked so well-tended and pretty. It was apparent that Duncan had taken quite a bit of care in planning the scenery, because it gave one a feeling of peace and solace when walking along the garden path. She also had to admit that he was very good looking to say the very least. He had a kind smiling face, and when he invited her back to the church, she could not help but want to return to that peaceful place. It was true enough that Delilah felt fine praying in her daily life, and at Amish services, but there was just something about St. Mary's Church that was comforting in a new and unfamiliar way. She decided to wipe these thoughts from her mind, and go about the myriad of chores that had to be done before dark. Daydreaming was not going to get her anywhere.

The following morning, the neighbor, Farmer Todson, came by in his buggy to say he was going back into the Englisch town to pick up an order he had placed yesterday. He wanted to know if we needed anything, and sure enough Deborah gave him a list of supplies that she and Ben required,

"Bruder Todson, could you please pick up these items from town? Delilah, why don't you accompany Bruder Todson, so that you can pick up our items while he conducts his own business. It wouldn't be fair to impose upon your time. We know how valuable time is when everyone is trying to restore things back to normal after the storm," declared Deborah. Delilah was actually grateful for the time away from her sister's farm, and she knew her mamm was in good hands with her younger bruders, so she agreed to accompany Farmer Todson. Plus, she might even get the opportunity to visit the church for a moment or two if she got the spare time. She climbed up into the buggy, and off they went towards Englisch town. She waved goodbye to her sister and Jonny, who stood beside her, and looked forward to a day away from the drudgery of her everyday life.

The ride into town was relaxing, with the trees and outlying pastures slowly recovering from all the wild winds of the last month. The trees swayed softly in the light breeze, and the sun was shining, making her feel nicely warm, and drying up the previously muddy roads. They arrived in town, and she departed from Farmer Todson. They agreed to meet back at the buggy in three hours, since he had much business to conduct with some of the Englischers. Delilah trotted off to the general store to pick up the odds and ends that Deborah had put on the list. She found all of the items quite quickly, and discovered that she had two more hours to spare before needing to meet at the buggy. She knew at once where she would love to spend that time! She hurried down Main Street towards St. Mary's, and found the church to be unlocked just as Duncan had said. Delilah sat down once again on the front pew, and marveled at the peace and quiet surrounding her. She said a few silent prayers from her heart, and then decided to take a leisurely walk around the grounds. All that she sought was some solitary moments by herself, because she certainly never got to enjoy any back home. As she wandered the grounds, she pondered what kind of life she might have somewhere different? She tossed around the absurd idea that she could ever leave the Amish fold, as few did, and Deborah surely needed her help. If only she was free to fly away like the bluebirds she saw fluttering amongst the garden. She suddenly felt very foolish thinking these preposterous thoughts, and quickly turned her attentions towards the little family of squirrels ahead of her. They looked happy enough. Delilah wished she could be happy too, and despite that promise she had made to herself of a solitary life, she still felt a nagging sensation that it sounded a rather lonesome option.

After about thirty minutes of admiring the flowers, squirrels and other critters, she spotted the tall, defined figure of Duncan in the distance. He was busy repairing what looked to be an old tool shed. Delilah noted his blonde hair, broad shoulders, and recalled the warmth that had radiated from his big brown, soulful eyes. For some reason, Duncan kept making unwelcome appearances in her daydreams, and now here he was right in front of her. She tripped on a twig, making a snapping noise, which caused Duncan to look up from his labors. He smiled brightly, and placed his tools on the work bench beside him. Delilah's heart skipped a beat, as she saw him approaching her. What would he possibly want? After all, he was a handsome, hardworking Englischer, and she was part of the Amish. They existed in two different worlds. She had willingly declined to take part in Rumspringa, thinking there was no point in participating. It had seemed like a luxury that she could not afford, because Deborah had been desperate for help when Delilah had been at age to participate. All this panic backtracking did not matter now, as Duncan approached where she was standing. Before she could think straight, Duncan was upon her, talking in his usual cheerful way,

"Well, hello again, Miss Delilah! What brings you back so soon?"

"Hello, Duncan. I trust you have been well this short time?"

"Yes, I have been working away as normal, but I must confess, I was thinking of you just yesterday, wondering when I'd have the pleasure of meeting you again! And here you are! What a lucky coincidence," laughed Duncan. His manner seemed so different from the other men that she had grown up with. Abner and Benjamin had never spoken with such relaxing ease, or had seemed so sincere. She wondered what to make of Duncan. She had had little contact with other Amish young men, having steered clear of courting. Could young men be forthright and good? Delilah was torn between acceptance and mistrust, as she contemplated what to make of the young man. As if reading her unsure mind, Duncan invited her to sit a spell,

"Miss Delilah, please, won't you come sit and rest yourself in the prayer garden? I don't believe you have seen that portion of the grounds yet. You must come see it. I think you'll find it inspirational, and you look as if you could use some refreshment. Allow me to fetch some cold water, and you can relax a bit."

"I guess that would be alright," and at that, Duncan led her, mindful to behave in a gentlemanly manner, to the partially hidden prayer garden. It sat back behind the shed, along a cobblestone walkway,

"Well, here it is! This is where many people come for prayer and reflection. It is a lovely spot that I designed just a few months before the storm. I'm rather happy with the way it turned out. You see the pond there, beyond the benches, and the statuary I purchased," explained Duncan.

"It is so lovely here!" declared Delilah. Duncan gently suggested that she take a seat and make herself comfortable, while he went back to the cabin for some refreshments. Delilah did just that, and chose a pretty mosaic bench situated between two angelic statues that seemed to guard over the prayer garden. It was such a magical little place! Imagine coming here every day to sit and reflect with Gott. She was almost sure that her Amish Gott would approve of such a peaceful and reverent setting in which to pray, and enjoy the beauties of nature. Duncan had certainly outdone himself creating this oasis of calm just behind the main church building. As she sat admiring her surroundings, which were so foreign from what she was accustomed to, Duncan returned with a tray loaded with drinks and sandwiches! However did this man manage by himself, she thought with surprise! It was completely bewildering to her that a man could live all alone in such a setting, plus prepare his own food. Duncan surely appeared to be quite self-sufficient and industrious! She tried not to stare at his handsome frame, as he set the tray down upon a small stump that served as a table. Duncan was the most interesting man she had ever met,

"Thank you for all of this, Duncan! I didn't expect you to go to so much trouble on my account. A drink of water would have been more than sufficient. This is so thoughtful of you!"

"No trouble at all, Miss Delilah, especially for one as beautiful as you," Duncan said, before he realized what he had said, and the both of them blushed at the unexpected compliment.

"Oh, uh, thank you, Duncan, but I am just a simple girl. I am far from beautiful I am certain!"

"Quite the opposite, Delilah. I am so happy that you are here again today. I wanted to show you this spot the last time you were here, but time got away from us. I hope you consider it a lovely place?"

"Quite!" Delilah replied, as she took the mason jar filled with lemonade that Duncan offered. It was delicious and sweet, and she felt happier than she had ever felt in her life. Not that that was a challenge, given her dismal past, "Duncan, it amazes me that you create such beauty, and yet you live all alone with no one to care for you..." She was not sure that she had said the proper thing, but it was a strange way to live according to her Amish traditions. The two of them sat together for the rest of her remaining time before having to meet Farmer Todson. They spoke about just about everything from Gott to gardening, to the similarities and differences between their two faiths. Duncan was a good and proper Christian man, and he told her how rewarding it was for him to live here in his modest cabin, caring for the good of the parish. She learned that nothing brought him more contentment than serving the Lord in his own way, using his own talents. He loved caring for the animals around the property, but did admit he felt a bit lonesome some of the time with the lack of human contact that went along with his duties. As the conversation came to a natural and easy end, Delilah noted that it was time to return to the buggy. She found herself wishing that she could stay longer. She had never before had a real companion with which to talk and share ideas and dreams. There was no time to ponder this new-found friendship, if that is what is was, as she was in a hurry to meet up with Farmer Todson. It was getting late in the afternoon, and the sin was beginning to set. It made for an enchanting scene, glimpsing the sun set along the horizon!

"Delilah, please allow me to walk you back to the buggy, as it is growing late, and you should not be unaccompanied in the street at this hour," Duncan prodded. She felt herself delighted and giddy at the thought of walking through town in the company of Duncan. He gently took her arm in his, and they proceeded along the cobblestone path back towards the front of the church,

"Thank you for a nice afternoon, Duncan. I hardly expected to have such an enjoyable visit with you today. It was certainly a pleasant surprise." Delilah couldn't help the rosy blush that colored her cheeks as she walked arm in arm with Duncan down Main Street.

"On the contrary, Miss Delilah, the pleasure was all mine! I do hope to see you again very soon. I don't suppose I could come calling on you at your home in the village? I am an Englischer, and would probably not be welcome as a visitor," said Duncan, but what he really felt was that he wanted nothing more than to become her suitor. In his eyes, Delilah was the most beautiful and angelic creature he had ever laid eyes upon. If only she was attainable, he thought rather sadly. He wished there was some way that they could continue their meetings in the purity of the church yard without the wagging tongues of outsiders both in the Englisch town and Amish village. This was going to be a tricky endeavor, but Duncan was smitten. It was all he could do to keep from grasping her hand in his as he said farewell before reaching the buggy. He felt that perhaps Delilah was as enamored of him as he was of her, considering they had just met a few days ago. Duncan was of a mind that once you found that special someone, that it was only proper to follow one's heart! He knew he must act cautiously, as Delilah seemed attached to her Amish way of life.

Along the bumpy journey home to the village, Delilah hardly said a word in conversation with Farmer Todson, as her heart and mind were filled with memories of the happy times she had passed with Duncan. He was the complete opposite of the men in her life. He was nothing like her father, Abner, or Benjamin, the laze-about, no good bruder-in-law! She was well aware of her aversion to men, and her desire to live alone, but Duncan had somehow ignited a fire within her soul! She longed to visit him again, but how? All she knew was that as soon as she arrived back home, she was going to confide in her schwester, Deborah. Perhaps there was some way to work things out, so the stirrings of her heart could be stilled. She knew by the look in Duncan's eyes that he felt an attraction towards her. It was almost too much excitement to bear! Was she getting her hopes up only to be disappointed, filled with the characteristic heartbreak of her mamm and schwester? Or could she dare to dream for a better life? Her head spun with so many questions, and she longed for the touch of Duncan's strong arms, as she recalled how walking arm in arm had sent shivers of delight up and down her spine! Everything seemed new and hopeful, and she dared not dwell too much on what the future had the potential to hold for her. The buggy jolted to a stop in front of her farm, and Farmer Todson bid her farewell as she clambered down, laden with Deborah's requested packages. She realized that she was practically running towards the house, and corrected her gait as she spied Benjamin clumsily stacking hay bales. He seemed wholly incompetent compared to Duncan. She felt sorry that Deborah was beholden to such a man, but put her thoughts aside as she entered the house.

Deborah had been hard at work, preparing the evening meal. With her bruders getting older and more mature, she saw in them a better work ethic than what they had been shown by their father while growing up in an unhappy home. She gazed at Miriam, her mother, who appeared to be complacent with her life with Deborah and her bopplis. Even Jonny, her faithful hund, seemed relaxed by the fireside. He was thrilled to see the return of his mistress, however, and ran to greet her with wunderbaar kisses! Delilah decided that the best time to approach Deborah and her mamm was after supper, once the children and Benjamin (whose habit it was to turn in early) were snugly in bed. Her plan was quickly formulating in her mind, and she hoped against hope that the most influential women in her life would approve of what she was about to propose. It was to be a gamble to be sure, but he knew in her heart that what she truly wanted was a different life than what the Amish community was able to provide. The Amish life had been a decent life, apart from the obvious unhappy home life, but now that she had met Duncan, and found how much she relished the Englisch ways, she wanted nothing more than to experience every part of it for herself.

Meanwhile, back at the church, Duncan sat in his cabin with a cup of hot coffee, thinking of nothing but the lovely and captivating Delilah. Her manner was so innocent, and her beauty surpassed any of that of any girl he had ever laid eyes upon. Did he dare to dream that she could possibly share a life with him in his Englisch world? He could not bring himself to force her to make a choice between two worlds that were seemingly so disparate. True, they worshipped the same God, as Christians, but Amish and Englisch did not intermix that way. It seemed to be a question of either a life with him in his world, or a life devoid of her presence in his life. Never had he been more keenly aware of how lonely he had felt than at this moment. Of all the young women in the town, why was it the unattainable Delilah that stole his heart? What was he to do if he never saw her again? He dared not think of the heartache he would feel if he was to live devoid of her easy laughter and innocent view of the world. She seemed to want nothing more than the basic simplicities of life, and he felt that once enough time together had passed, that he could create a wonderful life for the two of them.

After the evening meal had been cleaned up, and the children sent to bed, Delilah suggested that her mamm and schwester sit down for a talk in front of the fire. She prepared tea for them, and rehearsed in her mind how she wanted to say what she feared was the impossible. She wanted to leave. Her mind was made up. The promise that she had made to herself to swear off men was no longer her strongest wish. Despite her burgeoning affections for Duncan, she wanted to exist in the Englisch town, and perhaps find work at the church as a maid to the reverend or an assistant at the bakery amongst the heavenly scent of cream puffs and fresh pastries. She resolved to make her own way in life, but she would not give up her dedication to Gott. For it was through her prayers to Him that brought her to this important fork in the road, and she felt she could worship the Lord whether she practiced the Amish faith or the outside Christian ways like Duncan. She gazed at the women by the firelight, and prayed that they would give her permission to embark upon her own life. She would of course, visit as often as she could, and hoped that her family could also visit her in Englisch town. She finished preparation of the tea, and made her way toward the comfort of the hearth. Delilah wasted no time in launching into her desires, awhile her mamm and Deborah seemed to listen with no apparent judgment. As the discussion, or rather speech, came to an end, her mamm took Delilah into her arms, and cried tears of mixed emotions,

"Delilah, my dear maedel, you must follow your heart, despite how we will miss you. You have been a loyal daughter and have never uttered a word of complaint at the hard life we have been dealt. Not all men are like Abner or Benjamin! You must go to the Englisch, and make a new life for yourself, amongst the community that will make you a happy woman. If we stand in your way, you will come to resent us in time, and that is no way to live your life, my dear daughter. I have always wanted nothing but the best for you and Deborah," offered her mamm. Delilah was in tears as her mother accepted her unorthodox choice, and Deborah, although with a look of trepidation in her worn face, agreed readily with their mother. They both wanted nothing in the world more than for Delilah to have a happy and fulfilling life. And if this meant that she must leave the Amish village for a new start, then they would support her in any way that they could. The three women embraced and shared lots of tears of happiness and relief. It was decided that Farmer Todson would take her to Englisch town the next week, once she obtained work, and a decent place to live. Farmer Todson had many reliable contacts in town, and Miriam was trusting that he would use his best judgment in securing her daughter a proper place within the community. Deborah held Delilah in her arms for what felt like an eternity, and finally the three retired to bed, for there was much to do for Delilah's journey in the coming days.

The following week, Delilah was secure in her new position at the bakery, which she loved, and it was to the absolute surprise and joy, that Duncan learned of this turn of events. It was the miracle he had been praying for. God had answered his many earnest prayers that Delilah would somehow someday be his! At the end of her first day at the bakery, Duncan was waiting just outside to walk her to her lodging at Mrs. Albright's bed and breakfast. The two young lovers walked arm in arm in the moonlight towards her new home, and Duncan dreamed of the day when it would be appropriate to ask for her hand in marriage! Each held on to the dreams n their hearts that love and happiness were possible after all was said and done. There was so much to be thankful for, and their blessings many fold!

AMISH LOVE AT THE LAKE

ABBY BARKER

<u>Damn.</u>

Sadie felt bad even thinking the word, but she couldn't come up with anything else that summed up what she was feeling so completely. Standing on the edge of the lake that borders the small community where she's spent her entire life, she anxiously twisted the small diamond ring that felt like a vice on her finger. The rock sparkled in the sunlight with each rotation.

"Damn," Sadie whispered.

She'd only been engaged for about an hour, but it already felt like an eternity. She knew from the moment Matthew got down on one knee in front of all their friends and family that she didn't want to say yes. So, why was that the word that came out of her mouth? Her mother's happy tears and her sisters' excited tittering about how they would be next all but sewed her mouth closed when she tried to take it back. Matthew was an undeniably kind man, but that's all he was to her. Sadie wanted, no, needed something more and now it was too late.

She plopped down on the shore and pulled the ring off her finger and held it in her palm. A cool breeze came off the water and blew across her bare arms sending a chill down her spine. She felt more from that breeze than she ever did with Matthew. Sadie pictured his face reflecting off the water, his always-too-sincere smile plastered annoyingly on his face. She knew it wasn't fair, but after a while every time he asked her, "What's wrong, sweetie?" when she was in a bad mood she'd lash out at him because of that stupid smile. He never got angry, which only made her angrier. She wished that just once he would raise his voice, or storm off, or something other than mindlessly smiling at her. All that pent up anger bubbled up in her now as she raised her hand over her head to throw the ring into the water, but before she could do it a hand wrapped itself around her wrist.

"Whoa! If you don't need that ring anymore I'd gladly take it off your hands. It would be a waste to toss something so valuable into the depths."

Sadie looked up at the man who still held onto her arm. Even at such an awkward angle she could still tell that he was incredibly attractive. Dressed in a casual blue suit that hung smartly on his well-built frame, he had deep green eyes that matched the lake water sprawling out in front of them. He smiled down at her, but there was a hint of mischief in it, some depth that she couldn't quite pin down. A chill ran down her spine once more before she quickly pulled her hand out of his firm grip. The man chuckled.

"I didn't mean to startle you. I was just, sort of...walking along when I saw you about to toss away what looks to me like a few hundred bucks and I had to stop you."

"You were just walking along?"

They both looked around them. Aside from the lake, they were surrounded by a cast open field sprinkled with a few clusters of trees. Her town was almost two miles to the east along the water's edge and the nearest English city could be seen a ways away on the horizon. The man looked at Sadie sheepishly.

"You caught me. You want the truth? I was on a blind date at a fancy restaurant over there," he gestured to the city, "and it was going terribly. Honestly, I've never been on a worse date. When she showed up the first thing she said to me was, 'You look nothing like Nancy described you,' with a scowl on her face. A scowl! I don't know why she didn't just leave right then. My theory is that she just wanted the free meal because for the rest of the night she just looked down at her cellphone and would only answer my questions with a 'yes' or 'no' if I was lucky. Mostly she just grunted. Eventually, I excused myself to go to the washroom and just never came back. Before I realized it, I was walking toward this lake and I didn't want to go back to get my car until I was sure she was gone. That's when I stumbled upon you. Actually, what are you doing out here?"

The question caught her off guard. He had been speaking so rapidly and with so much energy that she could barely keep up. It took her a moment to register that it was her turn to speak.

"Oh, um, this is where I come to think."

"And what are you thinking about?"

Sadie blushed.

"Sorry, I don't mean to pry. It's just not everyday you meet a beautiful stranger next to a lake."

Sadie's blush deepened. So, he thought she was attractive too. A small smile formed on her lips.

"It's okay. In all honesty, I got engaged today and instead of celebrating with my friends and family I ran off here."

"And why's that?"

She didn't know why she was telling him all of this, but something about this handsome stranger made her comfortable enough to tell him anything he wanted to know.

"I don't want to marry him. I only said yes because my mother expected me to. What is a young, Amish woman good for if she isn't a wife, right?"

"Man alive, you've had a much worse date than I have," he laughed a little, but not unkindly. "For what it's worth, I'm sure you have plenty to offer other than your hand in marriage. You're a person, aren't you?"

Sadie looked straight at him with tears in her eyes. It was the first time anyone had acknowledged her as more than just a potential wife. He matched her eye contact and didn't look away.

"What's your name?" she asked.

"Mark, and yours?" He stuck his hand out for a handshake. She met him in the middle.

"Sadie. Nice to meet you out here on the shores of this lake, Mark. I'm glad you were just walking along today."

It was his turn to blush. Mark smiled and turned away from her, placing one hand on the back of his neck. They both sat silently for a while looking out across the water. The silence wasn't uncomfortable. The pair enjoyed the peace of each other's company for a few minutes before Mark spoke up again.

"I should probably head back. I don't want them to tow my car. Things seem to be a little bit complicated for you right now, but I still think I'd really enjoy seeing you again, if you have the time."

"Oh, I don't think my fiancé would like that very much," Sadie held the ring up between her fingers for Mark to see. "It probably wouldn't be a good idea." She seemed to say the last part to herself.

Mark nodded and stood up. He held his hand out to Sadie for another handshake.

"Well, I'll see you around then, Sadie. And please, don't throw that ring into the lake. I know a great pawn shop in town where you can make a few extra bucks if you really do have your heart set on getting rid of it."

Sadie took his hand. "Thanks, I'll let you know."

He gave her a mock salute before turning back in the direction he came and walking away. He never turned back to look at her, but Sadie could tell that he wanted to, or maybe she just wanted him to. With a small sigh, she turned back toward the lake and slipped the ring back onto her finger. It felt even heavier on her hand than it did before.

Mark.

There wasn't anything particularly special about the name, but she liked the way it sounded in her head. Mark, Mark, Mark. A mark was a symbol or a sign, an indication that something had been there and left proof of its existence. A mark was a reminder. This man had left as fast as he came, but he definitely left something behind. Sadie felt a little guilty about these thoughts, a little embarrassed, but mostly she felt like she wanted to see him again. Why didn't she just get up and go with him? They could have finished the date he left together, enjoying each other's company, laughing at each other's jokes. That's the kind of relationship she wanted – one where she felt something more than content at their best and trapped at their worst.

But then she remembered her mother. Her sisters' faces appeared in her mind not long after. They depended on her. Her mother expected her to find a husband, start a family of her own, run a household. That's what a "good Amish girl" should do. Anything that differed from that future was unacceptable. And her sisters looked up to her to set an example. All they've ever talked about is who they're going to marry, how they'd decorate their first homes, what they'd name their children. To see their eldest sister embark on that journey would show them that they're next. If she didn't go through with the marriage they'd be devastated, discouraged from pursuing their own futures even. She couldn't let that happen.

Sadie wasn't against marriage, by any means, she was against the expectation. Her sisters wanted to be married more than anything and she wanted them to have that. She just wasn't sure what she wanted for herself.

The sun had started to set over the lake and a chill was in the air. Sadie had been gone for hours. She'd lost track of time. Her family was probably worried sick, Matthew most of all. Annoyance bubbled up inside of her again thinking about his gently furrowed brow and comforting pats he'd give her mother while they worried about where she got off to. He'd say generically reassuring things like, "I'm sure she'll be back soon," and, "Don't worry. Sadie's a smart girl." The thought of him saying, "I'm so glad you're okay!" as he rushed toward her with outstretched arms made her want to scream.

She stood up and brushed the dried grass from her skirt, steeling herself for the walk back. At least she'd have another thirty minutes to herself on the walk home, forty-five if she walked slow. Sadie clenched her fists and set off along the shore in the direction of her town.

***

Sadie walked through the front door of her family home and was immediately met by a round of relieved gasps and a bone crushing hug from her mother. The woman was old, but not weak.

"Sadie! Where have you been? We were all so worried. After Matthew proposed you just left without a word. Where did you go?"

Sadie pried her mother off of her body.

"I just went for a walk, is all. I wanted to be alone with my thoughts to process everything for a while," she forced a smile. "I was overwhelmed."

Matthew walked over and took her hand, that saccharin smile goading her.

"My dear, I'm so glad you're okay. This is overwhelming! There's so much to think about and plan. I'm glad you took the time you needed, but next time will you please tell someone before you go?"

"Sure, dear," she pulled her hand out of his, "but now I'm very tired. I'd like to go to bed."

"Without dinner?" her mother prodded with concern.

"I'll eat in the morning."

Sadie was already walking toward her room before anyone could say another word. She shut the door behind her and leaned up against it. She knew her mother could tell something was wrong, she always could, but she didn't want to face it until morning, or later if she could help it. She moved to get ready for bed before she could sink to the floor and start wallowing again. She changed into her nightclothes and crawled under her sheets when a small but enthusiastic knock came at the door. They hardly waited for Sadie to say, "come in," before her two sisters barged through the door and hopped on the end of the bed.

"Sadie, can we see the ring again?" her youngest sister Molly asked, bouncing up and down the whole time.

"Oh yes, please, can I try it on?" her middle sister Amy agreed.

Seeing her sisters smile was always contagious, no matter the circumstances. Sadie grinned at them and slipped the ring off her finger.

She was happy to be free of it and to let them play out their little proposal fantasies with an authentic prop. Molly grabbed the ring and jumped off the bed, falling to one knee. Amy swung her legs off the side to face her. Molly cleared her throat and dropped her voice in an impression of the handsome and eligible bachelor that occupied their thoughts.

"Amy, my darling dearest, my sun and my moon, my apple pie with an extra scoop of ice cream, will you marry me?"

Amy threw herself backwards on the bed squealing with delight and kicking her legs in the air before righting herself and gleefully accepting the proposal.

"Yes, oh yes! Of course I'll marry you."

She stuck her hand out to accept the ring, which Molly dutifully placed on her expectant finger. Both girls descended into fits of giggles while Amy waved the ring in the air to catch it on the candlelight. Sadie couldn't help but smile. These girls mattered more to her than anything else on Earth and seeing them happy was pure joy. When the laughing finally subsided, Molly climbed back onto the bed and Amy begrudgingly handed the ring back to Sadie.

"When will the wedding be?" Amy asked with her hands under her chin. Both girls looked up at her expectantly from the foot of the bed.

"I'm not sure, but I bet Matthew would rather it happen sooner than later." Her stomach dropped at the thought. Matthew wouldn't want a very long engagement. The sooner they were married, the sooner he'd have someone to keep his house in order and make supper for him every night. The sooner they were married, the sooner they could start a family. The color must have left Sadie's face because she could see the concern on her sisters'. She smiled to dissuade their worry.

"I can't wait to fall in love," Molly said to no one in particular. Playing with her hair she turned to Sadie. "When did you know you were in love with Matthew?"

Sadie took a breath. She didn't want to lie to her sisters but she wasn't about tell them the truth either. She thought back to the time they first met. It was only a couple weeks after her twenty-third birthday when her mother surprised her one night with an extra guest at the supper table. This wasn't the first time she had done so, but it was the first time she saw the smile that would plague her for the next few months. After introducing them, her mother went on and on about the family business Matthew was set to inherit and Sadie's most recent needlework project. "She's a master with a needle and thread, let me tell you. My girl could fix any tattered rag you put in front of her." She didn't bother mentioning her interest in astronomy or the fact that she never lost a foot race when she was younger because these things didn't make her a good wife, but they made her who she was.

Matthew just nodded along, agreeing with Sadie's mother every time she mentioned how beautiful or pious or dutiful she was. With each nod Sadie became more and more disinterested in him. By the time supper was over she had all but forgotten his name until her mother pulled her aside to talk.

"I think he might be the one, honey."

"And why do you think that, Ma?"

"Because he's still here! Sadie, I can't keep doing this. I'm getting old and tired and I just want to see you with someone who will take care of you."

"But I can take care of myself, Ma!"

"I won't have this argument with you again. Do you want the neighbors to talk? It would break mine and your father's hearts to watch you waste your life childless and alone. You're an Amish woman, Sadie. Act like it."

After that conversation, when Matthew asked if she'd like to see him again she had to say yes. Since then, they've gone on weekly dates and he'd give her rides home in his buggy after church every Sunday. She figured she'd eventually break up with him once her mother cooled down again, but the proposal came first. It caught her completely off guard and before she knew it she was engaged. She obviously couldn't say any of that to her two impressionable sisters, so instead she told them what they wanted to hear.

"The moment I looked into his eyes I knew."

The girls squealed.

"That's so romantic!"

"I hope that happens for me. I want to know right away. No questions."

"I'm so jealous of you, Sadie. You must be so happy."

Her fake grin began to falter.

"Yeah, I must be."

The girls chattered away for a while before heading off to their own beds. Sadie felt a little guilty for lying to her sisters, but not nearly as guilty as how she'd feel if she told them the truth. The thought of watching those excited smiles fall off their faces broke her heart. There had to be a way to avoid marrying Matthew without hurting her family. Sadie fell asleep that night plotting her escape.

***

In the morning she woke up to a knocking on her door. She tried to ignore it at first but it came again. When she told whoever it was to come in, Matthew walked through the door. Matthew didn't a habit of showing up at her home early in the morning, let alone in her actual bedroom. For the first time she can remember he wasn't smiling.

"Sadie, I wanted to give you your space but we need to talk about what happened yesterday." He sat down at the foot of her bed. "I understand that you needed some time to think, but you can't just go running off without telling anyone, especially me. I'm your future husband, I really should know where you are."

"You want to know where I am at all times? That's just not possible."

"It is possible and you know it. I want to know when you're in our home, or at the market, or visiting your family. I have to be able to take care of you, make sure you're okay, and I can't do that if you wander off."

"If I wander off?" She was getting angry now. How dare he barge into her home before she's even dressed and berate her like this. "I'm not a child, Matthew. I'm a grown woman and I will go where I please. I don't need your or anyone else's permission to 'wander.'"

"I know I've caught you off guard, now and with the proposal, but that doesn't mean we have to lash out at each other. I love you, Sadie. I just want what's best for you."

His calm and patronizing tone almost sent her over the edge. She sat up and kicked the covers off of herself, jumping out of bed and as far away from Matthew as she could manage.

"I think you should go, Matthew. We can talk about this later."

"Sadie..."

"Please. Just leave. I don't need to know where you go."

She had her back turned to him and her arms crossed. She couldn't bring herself to even look at him. Eventually, she heard the creaking of floorboards and her bedroom door open and shut. A sigh of relief escaped her lips. How dare he ambush her like this, and with such a ridiculous and controlling request? Did no one see her as the woman she was instead of just her potential to make a man happy? Sadie felt a tear run down her cheeks. She wiped it angrily away and started to get dressed. She felt cooped up and cornered. Matthew knew she was there and after the conversation they just had she needed to be anywhere else. Sadie pulled on her shoes, stormed out the front door, and walked toward the lake.

On her way she fumed about all the things that Matthew did that bothered her. His smile was number one. The way he folded his napkin into a perfect triangle after every meal really got on her nerves. That, and how much he talked about his older sister like she was the epitome of a good Amish woman. Even if she did end up marrying him, how was she ever supposed to live up to the idealized version of a woman that Matthew had cooked up for himself in his mind? Sadie was so lost in thought stomping along the shore that she almost didn't notice the man walking toward her from the opposite direction. When they got closer, she was shocked to find it was Mark. He didn't seem surprised at all, in fact, he seemed relieved as he waved at her when they had gotten closer.

"Sadie! It's you! And it's me. Do you remember me? I mean, it was only yesterday when we met so I hope you remember me."

Sadie couldn't hide the surprise on her face when he approached her.

"Yes, I remember you. What are you doing out here?"

Matthew laughed. "I had this whole excuse lined up about how I lost a glove or something and had to come back and find it but I didn't expect to see you this soon and I haven't quite perfected my story yet."

"Your story?"

"Yeah, about why I'm out here circling the lake. I didn't want you to know right away that I was hoping I'd see you again, but here I am unprepared." They stared at each other for a moment. Sadie didn't know what to say to him. "It's good to see you."

"You wanted to see me?"

"Yeah."

"And you thought the best way to find me would be to walk around this enormous lake until I showed up again?"

"It worked, didn't it?"

He had her there. Whether it was fate or something else, he did end up finding her again. She barely knew this man but seeing him in front of her know made her feel relieved. His hand was rested sheepishly on the back of his neck and he somehow looked up at her through his eyelashes despite being several inches taller. In spite of everything, she was happy to see him too.

"And what was it you planned to say to me once you found me?"

"See, I hadn't gotten that far yet either. But probably something about how beautiful I thought you were when I saw you sitting by the lake yesterday and how upset it made me feel to see the sadness in your eyes when I got closer. I'd probably say something about how you deserve better, Sadie, and you shouldn't be with a fiancé you don't love." He stepped closer to her. "I know we just met yesterday and we barely know each other at all, but I want to know you. There's just something about you that made it impossible for me to get you off my mind and, you know what, I don't want you to go."

Sadie felt like a wave had just come up out of the lake and crashed over her entire body. Her knees went weak, but Mark had already grabbed her by the hands, holding her up. Every emotion that she never felt with Matthew – passion, surprise, heartbreak – rushed through her veins. This man was a stranger to her just the day before, and for the most part still was, but now she looked into his green eyes and saw depth; in his eyes was the potential for so much more. But what about her family? Sadie yanked her hands out of Mark's soft grip.

"I can't."

"What do you mean? Of course you can. You're your own person."

"You don't understand, Mark. You said it yourself, you don't know me and you don't know my family. I have to marry Matthew, an Amish man, or else I'll shame my entire family. The only thing worse than not marrying at all would be marrying an English man."

But her words didn't discourage Mark. He grabbed her by the waist and pulled her into him. One hand moved up to the nape of her neck, fingers entwined in her hair. He held her there for a moment, looking straight into her eyes.

"Tell me you don't feel this too. Tell me and I'll turn around, walk back to my car, and forget this lake is even here."

Sadie didn't say a word. Without even thinking, she closed the gap between her and Mark. Her lips found his as she wrapped her arms around his muscular torso and pulled him tighter. She felt his hand pull her face into his, their bodies tensing and relaxing like the lolling water behind them. The kiss seemed to last forever, but end too soon at the same time. The pair stood holding each other and catching their breath for a moment before Sadie gently pushed Mark away from her.

"I shouldn't have done that."

She put her fingers to her lips. They still tingled from the kiss, but that warmth was overwhelmed by feelings of guilt. No matter how she felt about Mark, she was still engaged to Matthew. But what did this mean? Was she ready to break it off with Matthew all for the chance at love with a man she hardly knew? The way he was looking at her at the moment overwhelmed her. She began to back up, unsure of what she should do next. Mark took a couple steps toward her, arms outstretched, with a concerned look now in his eye. This only made her back up faster. Suddenly, she felt the land fall away from beneath her feet and the icy embrace of the water take its place. In her panic, Sadie accidently walked into the lake.

Mark wasted no time jumping in after her. The water wasn't very deep and Sadie had spent every summer of her childhood swimming laps in the very same lake, but he had no way to know this. Once in the water, Mark swept a thrashing Sadie up into his arms and pulled her out of the chilly lake. He stood there in the waist-deep water for a moment before walking them both to the shore. He gently placed Sadie on the bank before climbing out of the water and plopping down next to her. Despite the chill, Sadie's cheeks were flushed red from embarrassment.

"The kiss was that bad, huh?"

Sadie hid her face in her hands until she peeked out from between her fingers to see that he was teasing her.

"No! I don't know what that was. I'm so sorry. I guess I thought you were going to try to kiss me again and I wasn't ready for that. This is all very overwhelming for me."

"I get it. It's pretty overwhelming for me, too. Not dive-into-a-lake-fully-clothed overwhelming, but I've never felt this way, this fast about someone before. I can see you need some time to process this, and to dry off, but I want you to know how serious I am." He wrung out his jacket as best as he could and draped it over her shivering shoulders. "Part of me thinks my date yesterday was meant to go poorly. If it wasn't so terrible, I never would have walked out to the lake and I would have never met you. I can't imagine sitting across the table in a fancy restaurant from another woman who makes me feel the way you do when I look at you. Go back home, think about what you want, what you deserve. I'll be here, right in this exact spot tomorrow at sunset. If you show up then I'll know you want to see where this goes, too. If you don't, then I'll never come back here."

Mark stood up and offered Sadie his hand. She took it and he pulled her to her feet. Her hand lingered in his for a moment before she pulled it away. She looked at Mark and nodded. He was right, she did need some time to sort her thoughts out. Two days ago she never expected to be in this situation. She didn't know what she was going to do, but she did know she needed to change out of her wet clothes. Mark gave her one last smile before turning around and walking back towards the city. Sadie wanted to say something, but she didn't know what. She couldn't reassure him that she'd be back, and anything else felt wrong, so she stayed silent and watched him slowly walk away before finally doing the same.

***

Back at home, Sadie locked herself in the bathroom and drew herself a warm bath before any of her family members realized she was home and asked her where she'd been. She undressed and looked at herself in the mirror. Her dark brown hair was still damp from the lake water, the stringy locks draping down over her pale shoulders. Unclothed, she could see herself as woman unburdened by labels like "wife" or "Amish." In this purest form she could about her wants and desires as her own, separate from her family's expectations of her.

Sadie stepped into the bath and sunk into the water. The experience was much more pleasant than her accidental bath earlier. She submerged her whole head underwater and held her breath. Under the surface, everything was silent with the exception of her heartbeat thumping in her ears. She tried picturing Matthews face in her mind, but all she could see was his mouth, upturned and taunting. Could she really spend the rest of her life with a man whose entire being made her blood boil? Her mother's face took the place of Matthew's smile. Her wrinkled eyes looked back at her with love and worry. Sadie burst through the surface of the water with a gasp. She'd made up her mind.

After drying off and putting on her clothes, Sadie walked down the hall to the bedroom her sisters shared. She knocked on the door before stepping inside. The two girls were sitting on Molly's bed, Amy braiding her sister's hair while they both laughed at some inside joke. Sadie sat down on the empty bed with a nervous energy. Her sisters picked up on it right away.

"What's the matter, Sadie?" Amy asked, her fingers still braiding away.

"Yeah, you look upset. Where did you go this morning? Did something happen?" Molly followed up.

Sadie wrapped her arms around herself and looked down at her lap. She was afraid of how her sisters might react to what she was about to tell them.

"Amy, Molly, I'm not in love with Matthew. I'm sorry I lied to you, and to everyone, actually, including myself."

Amy dropped Molly's hair and swung around to face her older sister. "What do you mean? Are you still marrying him?"

"No. No, I can't do it. I don't love him. I don't even like him. He's a fine man, but not the one for me. I only started seeing him in the first place because Ma was afraid I'd never get married. And you two were so excited when Matthew proposed, I didn't know how to say no."

"We're not the ones who have to marry him, Sadie! We were excited because we thought you were. I might be young, but I do know one thing for certain. A women shouldn't marry a man she isn't in love with. That's what getting married is all about, isn't it? Love."

Sadie was floored by the wisdom Amy seemed to had. She'd underestimated her sisters. Marriage was about love – the love between man and wife, the love that brings their families together, the love that their community showers on the new couple. Her mother would understand why she didn't want to marry Matthew because she loved her, and she would love Mark for the same reason.

Sadie got up off the bad and walked over to her sisters. She wrapped them both up in a huge hug.

"I love you two."

"We love you too," said Molly. "You're the best. I'm sure someone way better will come along soon anyways."

The girls were quick to notice the blush that crept across Sadie's cheeks. Their eyes went wide.

"You already have met somebody new! Who is he? Does he live in town? Is he handsome?" A river of questions flowed out of Molly's mouth.

Sadie laughed. "I'll tell you about him soon, but first there are a few things I need to take care of."

She gave the girls one more squeeze before walking out into the hall. She started for the front door, ready to walk across town to Matthew's house when she noticed him at their kitchen table. He was sitting there with her mother and a cup of tea in his hands. When he saw her, he stood up and rushed toward her.

"Sadie, I'm so sorry about our argument earlier. I don't want to fight with you, especially before we're even married. Can you forgive me?"

"Yes, I can forgive you, but I can't marry you."

Matthew's face fell and his arms which were on their way to embrace her fell to his side. Her mother jumped up from the table.

"What are you talking about, Sadie? What do you mean you can't marry him?"

"I mean exactly that. I'm not in love with you, Matthew. I'm sorry that I let you believe I did, but I felt trapped." She turned to her mother. "Ma, I don't want to disappoint you and Pa but I don't want to be unhappy either. I'm more than your daughter, or a wife, I'm a person with her own hopes and dreams and feelings."

Tears fell from her mother's eyes. "Sweetheart, I didn't know you felt that way. You know I only wanted the best for you. I thought that was marrying Matthew, but if that's not how you feel then I don't want you to do it. You and your sisters and your father are the most important people in my life, which makes your happiness important to me too. I love you, Sadie."

All the while Sadie and her mother were talking, Matthew stood silently to the side, but now he had something to say.

"I've got to say, Sadie, I'm surprised. I did mean it when I proposed to you, but I'm not about to ask you again to do something you don't want to do. These past couple of days have been tumultuous and if that's any indication of what our marriage might be like then it's probably for the best we aren't going through with this."

Matthew stuck one hand back out for a polite handshake. Sadie happily returned the gesture. He turned to leave, but before he could make it out the door she ran after him. She slipped the small, golden ring off her finger and handed it to him.

"I almost threw this in the lake. I'm glad I didn't. That ring was made for some other woman. Keep it."

When he smiled back at her this time she didn't feel annoyed. Matthew put the ring in his pocket and walked out the door. Sadie felt weightless for the first time since she was a child floating on her back in the lake looking up at the sky. She knew exactly what she wanted now and she was excited to find it on the shore of that very same lake the next day.

THE AMISH GROOM

ELAINE JOY MILLER

Lovina rolled over in her cotton sheets and stared out the window at the sun beaming through the ragged curtains of her bedroom. The light from the morning lit up the interior of her modest room. The cock crowed as she stirred and stepped from the comfort of the warm bed. As her delicate toes touched the floor she winced at the feel of the cool floorboards beneath her feet. She mentally prepared herself for another typical day in the remote Amish community where she was raised. She sat on the edge of her bed and began braiding her long, golden locks. Her hair had never been cut. Once finished she tied a tiny, white bow at the end. Standing up, her hair extended all the way down to her upper thighs.

From the homely bedside table, she grabbed her prayer cap, the white cap made of organza and stiff with starch that she must wear in public. She slipped it over her long, golden braid and stood, making her way over to the wardrobe, barefoot. The floorboards creaked beneath her slender frame. The house in which she lived was in need of much repair, but it was home.

Her dress was bound by the Amish community to which she belonged. She pulled out the calf-length, gray dress, and her white apron to accompany it. She looked the outfit up and down, sighing at the restrictions she had to abide by. Just a little color or a little lace would make it so much more tolerable, but alas it was forbidden.

She slipped the dress over her head, atop the white, cotton undergarments she wore beneath. Her slender arms penetrated the long sleeves at the ends and her delicate fingers stretched out toward the floor. Her blue eyes reflected in the full-length mirror that stood opposite. They ran over her entire frame, assessing the modesty of her attire. Her smooth legs peeked out the bottom of the gown. Her hands just protruded from the sleeves. How she longed for something different. To have somewhat more choice when it came to the little things. But living here her options were overly restricted. With a sigh, she turned away from her dull reflection.

Her stomach growled lightly, alerting her that breakfast time was upon her. Before leaving, she quickly raced to the window and opened it wide, allowing the cool morning air to hit her face. It almost stung as the contrasting wind nipped at her warm skin. She turned on her heels and made her way to the exit of her humble sanctuary, ready to start the day ahead.

Before opening the door she took a deep breath, hearing the faint clip-clop of hooves outside. She felt a tear well up in the corner of her eye, but she willed it to stop. No matter how much she tried, Lovina was overwhelmed with pain with any reminder of her parent's accident. No day since their passing had her parent's death become any easier for Lovina. Each day she was reminded of the terrible accident they had undertaken. As soon as she set eyes on the cart outside, laying rusted and disheveled. Unused for a year. A constant visual scar, sitting in their front yard. Although she knew that her brother, Jacob, shared her pain she would not dare discuss with him.

He had been walking down the street when it occurred. On his way back from the cornfields down the road from their home. Their mother and father waved as they passed, smiling at him. The next thing Jacob knew, he was watching their cart overturn as the horses bucked and bolted, leaving the two bodies trapped beneath the wreckage. Around him, people screamed at the sight, but all he could do was rush over to find his parents laying lifeless in the middle of the dirt road.

Lovina was distraught. She cried for weeks. She took to her room and moped. No one could comfort her. Since then the community had done their best to assist the two orphaned children. They stayed in the family home, but here they could barely make ends meet. Her job as a milkmaid at the dairy farm and his as an apprentice blacksmith left them living pay day to pay day. They relied on handouts from neighbors and friends to feed themselves. Still, Lovina and Jacob vowed to take care of themselves, and that was just what they did. Regardless of if it was against the rules.

One evening, months after the accident, Jacob had an idea. He weighed it up in his mind over and over. He had promised Lovina the day of their parents passing that he would always take care of her. That was just what he intended to do. But not if it meant risking her safety or standing within the community. Finally, he decided that there was no other option for them. The need for financial stability was too great.

"Come out with me tonight," he had asked, his voice trembling with what she felt to be nerves, excitement or worry, she could not distinguish.

"To where?" she had asked, but he would not answer. Lovina was wary at first of her brother's sudden plan. Still, she trusted him and so she followed, through the woods and to the city on the other side.

"Where are we going, Jacob?" she asked on their journey. He turned and held out his hand, signaling her to stop in her tracks. He opened the knapsack he had been holding tightly to his chest since they had left the community. Inside was a range of colorful clothing, the likes of which Lovina had never seen.

"I am taking you to the city," he explained, pulling out a pale pink fitted dress and white heels for his sister. She stared in awe at the strange fabric garments handed to her.

"You need to wear these, otherwise they will know we are not from there," he explained. Entering a modern city in their modest attire would surely give them away as patrons of the well-known Amish district just miles away. Jacob had experienced this prejudice first hand after all.

"I will stand over there. Let me know when you have changed. You can put your clothes in this bag," he gestured to the bag from which he had pulled the new outfit. Then he turned and walked out of sight, giving his sister the privacy to change.

She untied her apron and dropped her dress to the forest floor. She folded them and placed them in the knapsack Jacob had provided. She shivered in the cold night air. Picking up the new dress she pulled it gingerly over her head. It was so tight and firm around her body. She looked down at herself in the odd creation. Quickly she slipped the heels on her feet and called out,

"I think I am ready Jacob!" moments later he emerged from the shadows. He paused, taken aback by his sister's speedy transformation. He took her hand and kicked the knapsack into a large bush beside them.

"Time to go then," he whispered and they were off again through the trees.

When they came out on the other side of the vast wood, Lovina stopped in awe. The lights glistened in the distance as they looked over the high-rise jungle. Jacob had been lucky enough to experience life on the other side. This is where he had been during Rumspringa, but his freedom was short-lived. He promptly returned to the community, overwhelmed by the progression he experienced.

Lovina had not had that luxury. This was her first time in the city, even seeing it from a distance.

"Why are you bringing me here?" she mumbled. Jacob's expression became serious.

"We need money, Lovina. I did not want to worry you with such matters but since our parents passing we have been struggling... more than you know." she had no idea what this had to do with going to the city.

"We can get jobs here. Second jobs, at night. It has been so hard for us Annaliese and I need your help. Please," he begged. But she would do anything for her brother. She took his hand once more and squeezed it kindly.

"Then let's go," she said, excitedly.

Months later and they had been working at the diner quite regularly, almost every night. Lovina darted around in her short, yellow waitressing uniform, serving tables left and right. After her first day, she was amazed at how much money she had made, and just in tips. In the kitchen her brother worked hastily, cleaning dish after dish and piles of cutlery. But neither of them minded the hard work, especially Lovina. She was happy to just be out in the real world.

"Order up!" the chef boomed from the service window. He rang the bell relentlessly to alert her of food being ready to pick up. She scooted over and took it to her waiting customers. Now she had everything down to a fine art.

The sneaking around was getting quite cumbersome, however. Her heart raced each night her and Jacob ventured out, against the communities wishes. That night when she got home she collapsed on the bed and stared up at the ceiling. Exhausted, she wished her life was more simple. Leading her dual existence was taking its toll on her. She was plagued with a lack of sleep and a crippling anxiety. Tossing and turning during her few hours sleep each night. Alas, she had no other choice, for now anyway. She felt a huge debt weighing on her, for her brother. He had taken care of Lovina since their parent's sudden demise. No matter how much she wished she could leave, it was not an option.

One morning as she was walking down the street, Lovina was greeted by an unexpected face.

"Lovina!" a man's voice boomed from behind her. She turned quickly on her heel to see an old friend, one whom she thought had left for good years earlier.

"Jebidiah?" she said, stunned. Her grocery basket fell to the ground with a thud as she ran toward him and wrapped her arms around his broad shoulders. He picked her up around the waist and they held their embrace for several seconds. Even though it had been so long since their last encounter, neither failed to recognize the other.

He dropped her back to the ground and she stepped back slightly to take in the sight of her long lost friend. His hair was styled just as it always had been. His dark brown locks were cut short, a few inches from his scalp. It hung in waves around his face. His skin was tanned and contrasted perfectly with his strong, masculine jawline and muscular figure. His chin was littered with stubble, giving his face a slight shadowing.

Their last meeting had not been so joyous. Jebidiah had been leaving for Rumspringa with her brother Jacob. The three children had grown up as close as they could be, spending endless hours together playing in the cornfields and chasing each other through the streets. Since the age of five, Lovina and Jebidiah had known each other. She saw him as one of her closest friends. Or at least she had before he disappeared.

It had been a cold night, pelting down with rain. They stood there, facing each other. Lovina had been fifteen, Jebidiah sixteen. Not a word was spoken for several minutes between them. Too young to realize the deep feelings that connected them, Jebidiah left with Jacob, to experience the modern world with the rest of the community boys coming of age that year. Lovina had waited for him. She waited up at night and watched for him during the day. But he did not return.

Jacob came back weeks later with a few of the neighborhood boys, but Jebidiah was not among them.

Her brother had rested his hand on her shoulder as tears rolled down her face, tears for the loss of her best friend.

"He said to tell you he will see you again. He promised." at the time Lovina had not believed him. She had thought her brother was trying desperately to bring her out of her deepening hole of overwhelming sadness. But with Jebidiah standing before her, Jacob's words echoed in the midst of her thoughts.

'He promised.'

She had given up hope of seeing him again, yet here he stood, in the flesh.

Jebidiah was speechless. He had returned to the community after years. It seemed that no matter how much the modern world drew him, his love for Lovina was stronger. From the day he had left, he did not stop thinking about her, not for a moment. It had been fun and he savored the new experiences put forth by his peers in the city, but no one could replace her. That was what influenced him to return. There was nothing more he could gain from the city, he was looking to start a family. Jebidiah could not consider anyone else he would rather make a life with than her.

"I hope Jacob gave you my message all those years ago," he said, smiling down at her from above.

"He did," she replied, mirroring the beam that had taken over Jebidiah's face. Any onlooker could tell that these two were much more than just friends, even if they had not yet admitted it to themselves. They still grasped the hands of each other as they chatted for a few minutes about shared memories from the past.

Jebidiah bent down and picked up the discarded basket of groceries Lovina had dropped in her shock at his appearance.

"Let's go for a walk, I need to catch up with you. So much has happened in the last few years I am sure," he laughed. As they strolled along they spoke at length about their experiences. Everything Jebidiah said about his time away absolutely intrigued her. She desperately wished that she could share in this modern world, if only for a day. Working was all she had ever had the chance to do when her and Jacob managed to escape for their night shifts.

"So, what about your life, Lovina?" he questioned. After a moment of thought, he saw her face drop. The only significant thing she could think of to tell him was of her parent's sudden demise the previous fall. She took a deep breath and prepared herself for the retelling of the most painful memory she possessed.

"Actually, there was an accident last year," she began. Jebidiah's permanent grin faded almost immediately.

"My parents cart overturned. It was terrifying but the worst was that they did not make it." Jebidiah could not find the words to express his condolences. After a few moments to comprehend the brief and saddening story he mustered,

"I am so sorry, Lovina."

As always, her first thought was to change the subject, and so she did. Long ago she had decided that her parents would not have wanted her to mourn, but cherish the life that she had. That was exactly what she intended to do. The sadness they had been wallowing in for that brief moment evaporated quickly as they moved on to more trivial and light-hearted news from their vast time apart.

Jebidiah walked her all the way back to her door. He handed back the basket as she stepped through the threshold of the dark, polished doorway.

"Well, I am sure we will see each other again soon," he said as he turned to leave.

"You will," she smiled and with that the door clicked shut behind her.

As the following months flew by, Lovina found herself spending more and more of her limited free time with her long lost friend. Jebidiah found comfort in their closeness. Since moving back, he had faced endless scrutiny from the older members of the place he called home. They frowned upon him for his rash decision to leave, now that he had returned. He had known upon his abrupt return to his family that not everyone would be so welcoming. But no one else mattered as long as Lovina was by his side.

She found comfort in his company too. She was intrigued by his endless stories of the new technologies and strange architecture he had encountered in his years away. Unlike her peers, Lovina held nothing against him for leaving, if anything she wished that she could do the same.

The two companions spent their time just as they did, years earlier. Exploring the now familiar woods. Chasing each other through the cornfields. Collapsing with laughter on the dirt floor of the outdoors.

They savored each moment they spent in each others company. To Lovina, no one could compare to Jebidiah.

One sunny afternoon, they fell into each other's arms in the dewy grass of the outskirts of the boundary. Their laughter subsided and Lovina looked up at Jebidiah, beaming down at her. She knew that there was something deeper. This was not just another friendship, he meant so much more. Every second without him left her feeling cold and empty. Every second without her made him feel as if he was completely alone.

"Do you think you will stay here this time?" Lovina asked. She hoped that his answer reflected the way that she felt. But alas, he uttered the answer she did not want to hear.

"No. I think that now I have experienced what is out there, lived my life outside the confines of the community, I don't want to leave again." her heart dropped. There was nothing in the world she wished for more than to go, but a life without Jebidiah seemed just as empty.

It was his strength that encouraged her to plan her escape, to a new life in the modern world. Deep in her heart she knew that it was unlikely Jebidiah would come with her. After all, he had returned not weeks ago, but she had to follow her dreams. She had but one life, and she intended to live it. As much as she wanted to share with him her wishes, she knew this was one secret she must keep to herself.

Jebidiah walked her home again that day, as he often did of late. The sun was setting over the sovereign hills as they strolled past people and places on the way home. She took in the sights, for in a few weeks they would be gone forever. There was no doubt she would miss this place, but most of all she would miss him. She cherished the time they had together, though short lived.

They arrived at her home. Before she opened the door, Jebidiah grasped her wrist tightly. Her skin broke out in goosebumps all over in response to his flesh against hers. Her heart raced within her chest cavity. Cheeks began to glow red as the blood from her pounding heart rushed to her face. She hoped that Jebidiah did not see the intense reaction she gave from his touch.

"Do you have plans for tomorrow?" he questioned. His expression was serious all of a sudden.

"No," Lovina responded. Where was he going with this?

"I see, well goodnight then," he said with a grin. How strange. With that Jebidiah let go of her arm and placed his hands into his pockets.

"Goodbye," she called to him as he strolled slowly away, toward his family home at the end of the road.

As she closed the door behind her Lovina leaned her back against the rough wood and closed her eyes. The overwhelming sensation of lust she felt for Jebidiah was quickly blooming into a raging passion. Love. Little did she know that he felt it too. From the top of her head to the far tips of her toes her entire being was filled with admiration and desire for him. How would she tell him that she was going to leave the town? Start a new life in the place that he had run from.

She already had a plan in place. Two weeks from now she would be living amongst the modern world. Jacob had not been pleased, but he knew that he could not stop his sister from following her dreams. He had the opportunity, so there was no way that he could deny her that right, regardless of the community law.

"Are you sure you will be OK on your own?" Jacob could not hide the worried tone of his voice. Not even he could brave the new world, how could his little sister live there alone?

"I will, please do not worry about me, Jacob," then she explained her plan.

In the dead of night, while the town slept, she would sneak silently through the streets. Toward the wood. The path that they had traveled hundreds of times before would lead her to her new existence. She could not leave during the day, for fear of what scrutiny she may face from the others in the town. Women rarely left and were never welcomed home. It was best for her to just disappear.

"But you have never been that way alone." he said, his voice still trembling with fear for Lovina.

"I have mapped out our way. The last few weeks I have made a note of each landmark along the path. Each time I feel as if my feet lead me more and more. I step without hesitation." slowly she had memorized the way. Every rock and tree, branch and shrub. The dirt clearings and the overgrown mangling of tangled weeds, she was confident in her navigational ability. Even if Jacob was not so.

"Where will you stay?" his questions kept coming. But Lovina was not one to take her decisions lightly. To his every question, she had the perfect answer. During their time at the diner, they had made a few friends, both co-workers, and customers. Lovina had organized a room in a modest apartment with Katie, a fellow waitress at a neighboring restaurant. For only a small portion of her minimum wage, she had a place to her her own.

Several hours later, Lovina had assured her brother that she could fend for herself. If she ever needed him, he would be there for her too.

Jacob took her hand and looked at her, eyes full of sadness.

"I will always be here for you, sister," a single tear rolled down his cheek, winding its way through the stubble on his strong chin. Lovina was taken aback, she had not seen her brother so emotional since their parents passing. She whispered the only words that came to mind in response to his heartfelt confession.

"I know," tears now flowed freely down their faces. They sat in silence as Jacob took in the news she had revealed to him. The plan she had derived. How much he would miss her.

The hardest part was over. Lovina had dreaded telling her brother about her escape. Now she felt free, with his blessing she could leave without hesitation. She slept that night, soundly for the first time in many moons. Dreaming of the future adventures she would have in the big city.

The next morning Jebidiah was at her door before either of the siblings had risen. She heard the light tapping from her bedroom and quickly dressed to see who was so desperate to see them this day. She raced down the creaking steps and to the front door. Opening it widely she was ecstatic to see Jebidiah standing there with a bouquet of red roses. Their scent was swept immediately into her nostrils and she closed her eyes as the aroma intoxicated her.

"Good morning, Lovina," Jebidiah greeted her, placing the stunning bunch into her hands.

"Hello," she replied, staring at the gift he had brought for her. Something was different about him this morning. She could not pick it but his smile was strange somehow, brighter than she had seen before. His eyes sparkled in the morning light. Her heart skipped a beat as they paused for a moment, looking deeply into each other's eyes.

"I have a day planned for us," he said excitedly. Before she had time to properly lace up her boots, Jebidiah took her hand and whisked her away from her home. They walked together toward the vast cornfields at the end of the street. Waving at their fellow community members as they passed, Jebidiah led Lovina through the tall corn stalks.

She had no idea what he had in store. They rushed forward in silence. Lovina found her mind wandering as she took in the rays of sunlight winding through the stalks and leaves surrounding them. Her dress occasionally caught on rouge sticks and branches strewn throughout the fields. She stumbled a few times, but Jebidiah was there to catch her and help her find her feet once more.

Minutes passed and they finally arrived at the small clearing in the far end of the fields. Jebidiah let her hand drop and pulled a blanket from the backpack he had been lugging with them on the short journey. He laid it delicately out on the ground, straightening the edges and patting it down flat.

"Come, sit," he gestured to a soft spot on the blanket and she slowly approached, sitting down carefully, holding her dress flat against her thighs as she lowered her body to the ground. She watched on as Jebidiah began unpacking a picnic that he had prepared. She was stunned at the romantic setting that he had created for just the two of them, out of nowhere.

"I hope you're hungry," he laughed. Her eyes drifted from plate to plate, each piled high with sandwiches and cakes, fruit and salads. She could not believe what she saw before her. This was the kind of thing she had always dreamed of but had never eventuated into a reality. The sun beamed down on them as they began their conversations.

"Please," Jebidiah picked up a plate of her favorite sandwiches, fresh strawberry jam. She picked up one and took a bite. The sweetness of the jam found every corner of her tongue, leaving a lasting sensation in her mouth as she swallowed. He watched her intently, looking as if something was weighing heavily on his mind. Lovina looked into his deep, brown eyes. She felt herself smile as she took in his handsome features, just inches from her. His short, dark hair flowed subtly in the mild breeze. Her gaze followed his masculine jawline and rugged chin, covered in light stubble.

It was at that moment Jebidiah uttered the words she had been longing for him to say for so long,

"I love you, Lovina, I always have." she was taken aback. Of course, her heart reciprocated his feelings, but she could not bring herself to say the words back. In the back of her mind, she knew that if she revealed her love for him she must also let him in on the fact she was planning to leave. Leave him and everything else behind. Moments later she found her voice once more,

"I love you too."

They spoke for hours after Jebidiah's unexpected, but heartfelt, confession. Of life and the paths they wanted to take in the future. That was when troubles arose.

"I just want to settle down, and have a family. I love it so much here. It feels so right to be back." Jebidiah said in between bites of his rosy red apple. Lovina froze. This was exactly the life she was running from. It was the first time that she realized that their journeys may lead them in different directions. She sat silent for a moment as he waited patiently for her to say something, anything. She took a deep breath and proceeded to reveal her underlying plan to Jebidiah. Her plan to leave and start a new life in the city he had fled from.

"I had no idea," Jebidiah gasped, in response to her and Jacob's secret second existence outside of the community. His heart dropped as she continued to explain her plans to escape and live amongst the modern world. Never had he thought coming into the fields with her that morning that she would drop this bombshell upon him. All hopes of his quiet life back at home with his childhood sweetheart were slowly evaporating before his eyes.

"When do you plan to leave?" he questioned, his heartbeat pounding in his chest. He prayed that it was not soon. That he would have time to change her mind.

"Two weeks from today," she admitted. His smile had faded, and hers with it. She had thought that the hardest conversation before her departure was over, but she had not counted on Jebidiah's romantic notions. His proposal of a simple, family life in the mundane town she had always lived. She loved him deeply, but her want for adventure was overwhelming.

With the sun beginning to lower over the tips of the corn, they decided that it was time to return. She folded the blanket as Jebidiah picked up the empty plates that surrounded them in the clearing. He took her hand and led the way back through the towering stalks. They moved at a much slower pace upon their return. Lovina could not be sure, maybe it was due to the dimming light, but she felt as if their lagging pace was a bi-product of the conversations they had just had. Of her leaving him and the rest of her life behind.

Eventually, they reached her front door once more. She stepped up the front stair and peered down at him.

"Thank you for today, Jebidiah. I had an amazing time. I really appreciate all that you have done for me," Lovina checked quickly for onlookers and before a word could escape his lips she kissed him tenderly on the cheek. By the time Jebidiah realized what had happened she had already stepped back inside.

He began his journey home, filled with mixed emotions from the day just passed. He desperately wanted Lovina to stay, but he understood her position was difficult. With constant reminders daily of her parent's death, he could only imagine the heartache she must feel living here.

Two weeks later, the grandfather clock below the stairs began chiming midnight. Lovina knew this was her chance to make her escape quietly, without fear of waking her sleeping neighborhood. She tiptoed down the stairs, their echoing creaks masked by the gongs of the great timekeeper. Her blonde locks fell over her face as she looked down toward the door, her destination on this dark winter night. She brushed them aside and kept moving. Grabbing the already assembled knapsack from its hiding spot, she slipped her pale pink coat over her slender shoulders and on the final stroke of midnight the door clicked shut behind her.

The cool wind bit at her exposed flesh as she crept through the dead of night. She knew that by leaving she was breaking her oath to the Church, but the call of the outside world was just too great. Not even her one true love could keep her from following her dreams. A single tear rolled slowly down her pale cheek as she looked back, back at the friends and family she would no longer see. Back at Jebidiah.

Tearing her gaze away she strove forward. Her hair was now wet with sweat, despite the cold air that stung her face and pierced her lungs. She ran, as fast as she could. Each snapping twig made her heart jump. Every sound around her made her pause for a moment. A moment was all she could spare. Slowly she kept moving, through the woods, following the hidden road to freedom. As she made her way

Lovina found her mind wandering back to all of her most cherished memories with the community and everything she was giving up. The celebrations and family dinners. Just as she lost herself completely in her thoughts a sharp noise snapped her back to reality.

She looked around desperately for somewhere to hide. She could distinguish faint footsteps coming her way. Who could be out here this late, in the cold? Lovina was convinced that she was caught. Someone had overheard her speaking of her plan to Jebidiah, or worse he had outed her himself. She threw her knapsack into a large bush to her left and jumped behind. As she crouched on the ground crazy accusations filled her head, but she kept her blue eyes focused on the clearing before her. Was it Jebidiah who let slip her secret plan, or did someone else overhear? When a shadowy figure finally caught her eye in the woods, she waited with baited breath to identify her stalker.

Branches crunched beneath his feet as the man emerged into the grassy clearing, uncloaked by the light of the moon. Lovina's jaw dropped and her heart raced at what felt like a thousand beats a second. She no longer needed to hide, she no longer had any fear or doubt about the path that she had chosen.

"Jebidiah!" she exclaimed, sprinting as fast as her legs could carry her toward him. A smile exploded across his face as she jumped carelessly into his outstretched arms. Jebidiah wrapped his muscular arms around her. He grasped her as tight as he could, never wanting to part again. She let her body melt into his. There they stood, nestled in each other's arms for several moments before severing their sensual embrace.

"I could not let you go, Lovina. I love you." Jebidiah confessed. She stared into his beaming blue eyes, looking down upon her. There was only one thing that she could respond.

"I love you too," she answered. Her eyes welled up with blissful tears that soon began running, one by one, down her soft cheeks. Jebidiah reached forward and wiped them away with his calloused hands. One of her arms drew back, reaching up to run her fingers through his mess of tangled hair, damp with sweat. Still stunned by his sudden appearance, she was nothing but ecstatic to see him.

At that moment, Jebidiah leaned down and kissed her soft, cherry lips for the first time, basking in the cool blanket of moonlight penetrating the canopy. Lovina could not believe her luck as she stood in the middle of the trees, in the arms of her love. She had been sure, not hours ago, that she had lost the love of her life forever. Now, she was on her way to making a new life for herself, in a new world, with the man of her dreams.

She leaned in closer to his warm silhouette, grasping at the fabric of his coat. She savored his touch, something she thought she had lost forever in the sands of time. His hand brushed her now flushing cheeks. He traced down her neck and over her petite shoulder. Her hand found its place against his pounding chest. And hers against his.

Jebidiah brushed a lock of hair from Lovina's ear.

"We must go now," he whispered softly to her. Stepping back from him, she nodded in agreement. She would no longer need to start her new life alone, they were together at last. He picked up her knapsack and hauled it onto his back.

"Come," he ushered Lovina back onto her path. Toward the city for the last time. As they neared the bustling hub, she witnessed the blanket of light illuminating the town. Never had she seen something so beautiful. Never had she felt so free.